DATE DUE

AP 12 04			

Praise for Jay Bennett's previous suspense novels

DARK CORRIDOR

"Bennett has written another suspenseful novel, this time incorporating teenage suicide....Will definitely appeal to mystery fans."
—*VOYA*

THE HAUNTED ONE

"A poignant, gripping mystery which is hard to put down...Bennett is a master of psychological tension."
—*Midwest Book Review*

THE SKELETON MAN

"Bennett weaves his story with a deft touch and a high level of suspense that will keep young adult readers turning the page."
—*Los Angeles Times*

SING ME A DEATH SONG

"The rapid-fire dialogue...keep[s] the plot moving quickly....[Bennett] maintains the suspense and intrigue at an intense level throughout."
—*School Library Journal*

SKINHEAD

Jay Bennett

FAWCETT JUNIPER • NEW YORK

RLI: VL: 5 & up
      IL: 6 & up

A Fawcett Juniper Book
Published by Ballantine Books
Copyright © 1991 by Jay Bennett

All rights reserved under International and Pan-American Copyright Conventions. Published in the United States by Ballantine Books, a division of Random House, Inc., New York, and simultaneously in Canada by Random House of Canada Limited, Toronto.

http://www.randomhouse.com

Library of Congress Catalog Card Number: 90-13087

ISBN 0-449-70397-5

This edition published by arrangement with Franklin Watts

Printed in Canada

First Ballantine Books Edition: February 1992

For Iris,
with love

SKINHEAD

Chapter

1

The cold, insistent ring of the telephone waked him. He sat up in bed and then reached over to the night table and picked up the receiver. It glistened black in his pale hand.

"Yes?"

"Is this Jonathan Atwood?"

"Yes."

"I'm Sergeant Ward of the Seattle police."

"Seattle?"

Jonathan looked around at the shadowy walls of the huge bedroom. A ray of moonlight touched the ceiling, like a slender, silvery finger. Through the open windows, he could hear the soft, distant sound of the surf.

The voice spoke again. "I'm calling from a hospital. A man is dying and wants to see you."

"What man? I don't know anybody in Seattle."

"He wants you here before he dies."

Jonathan was silent.

"He won't give us his name," the voice said. "He was mugged and his wallet was taken. We don't know who he is yet."

"There is some mistake."

"No," the voice said.

Jonathan looked through the open windows to the white and gleaming beach. The moonlight lay flat and cold upon it.

He heard the voice again. "He knows you. Gave me your private phone number."

"How can he know me? I'm here at Southhampton, Long Island. Three thousand miles away," Jonathan said.

"He knows you. You're nineteen. A student at Amherst. You live with your grandfather, Peter Atwood. You're at one of your summer homes now. Does all this check out?"

Jonathan didn't answer.

Far out on the surf a wave flashed. And then it died. The water was broad and still again.

"Does it?" the voice repeated.

"Yes," Jonathan murmured. The hand holding the receiver trembled just a bit. And then became firm again.

The voice spoke once more. "I've done my job. It's up to you now. You can come out or not. He's at Colby Hospital. Room 601."

"You say he's dying?"

"He'll last a day or two at the most."

"Who is he?" Jonathan asked, and his face was white and taut.

2

"I told you we don't know."

"There's some mistake."

"Is there? Then let me run this by you. He says your grandfather is now in London heading up a conference of bankers. Is that so?"

"Yes," Jonathan said.

"Your father and mother live in Madrid."

Jonathan nodded slightly.

"Your father's been with our embassy for many years. Well?"

"That is so," Jonathan whispered.

There was a silence.

The sound of the surf came relentlessly into the room. Now it was louder. Beating like a giant drum. Beating. Ever beating. With an endless rhythm.

"Well?"

"I'll try to get a plane out," Jonathan said.

"Okay. Call me after you land and I'll meet you at the hospital."

"I will."

"Sergeant Tom Ward. 423-8200."

"Okay."

"Good-bye, Mr. Atwood."

Then Jonathan heard the click. He slowly put the receiver down, his eyes staring into the black, shattered night.

I'm scared, he said to himself.

"I'm scared," he whispered aloud.

"And I don't know why."

Chapter

2

After a while he rose and dressed.

Then he picked up the house phone and waited until a sleepy voice came on.

"Yes?" It was an old voice.

"Walter?"

"Is this Mr. Jonathan?"

"Yes. I have to go to Kennedy Airport," Jonathan said.

"Now?"

"Now. I need a morning flight to Seattle."

"Seattle?" There was a slight pause.

"Walter, did you hear me?"

"I did. Is anything wrong?"

Jonathan hesitated.

"Is there?" the old man repeated.

"I don't know, Walter. I got a call from a Detective

4

Ward that a man was mugged and wants to see me before he dies."

"A man? What man?"

"He won't give his name," Jonathan said.

"But he wants to see you?"

"Yes. Have you any idea what this is about?"

Again the pause.

"Walter?"

"It's very strange. Perhaps you should—"

"Will you arrange that flight for me?" Jonathan cut in.

"Yes, Mr. Jonathan."

"Good. I'm sorry to wake you. But it's urgent."

"I'll have Arthur come over with one of the cars," Walter said.

"If my grandfather should call, please tell him I went off to visit one of my college friends. Nothing more."

"I'll do that."

"Not a word more," Jonathan said.

"Yes."

"I'm sorry to have to wake you at this hour, Walter."

"Just have a safe trip, Mr. Jonathan."

"Thanks, Walter."

"A safe one."

And then he heard, "Perhaps you should call your grandfather and discuss it with him?"

Jonathan was silent.

"I'm sure he'd be glad to help," Walter said.

Jonathan was still silent.

"He's always there when you need him. He cares for you very much, Mr. Jonathan."

"I know that."

5

"Well?"

"Just set that flight up," Jonathan said quietly. He thought he heard the old man sigh.

"I will," Walter said.

"Good."

"You'll need a hotel reservation."

"Yes."

"You'll return?"

"The next day."

"Good-bye, Mr. Jonathan."

"Good-bye, Walter," Jonathan said gently.

He put down the phone and thought of the old, now white-haired man, and of the long years he had been in the Atwood household.

Walter held me in his arms when I was a small child. Lonely and lost. My father and mother always away somewhere. My grandfather eternally busy with his empire.

Walter comforted me.

Jonathan sat there thinking of those dim, haunted years.

And then the phone rang.

It was Arthur waiting in the car.

Jonathan rose and went out of the room, down the long, broad steps, and then out of the house. He stepped into the black limousine. The car sped off into the night.

Jonathan sat in the long, black limousine, looking straight ahead at the stiff, almost rigid form of the chauffeur. The man never spoke a word, even though they had known each other for many years. Not a word. A glass wall separated them.

Through my grandfather I have enormous wealth and power, Jonathan thought.

No one in this world can touch me.

No one.

Peter Atwood, my grandfather, stands like a stone tower before me and everybody else.

No one can harm me.

And yet I sit here in this huge car, alone and afraid. Of what?

Chapter
3

All through the flight to Seattle a voice within him kept saying, Turn back, turn back, Jonathan.

You're making a terrible mistake.

A fatal one.

When the plane lands, turn back.

Get into another one immediately.

Return to Southhampton.

To the brilliant sun on the beach.

And the easy, lush summer life coming up.

Each hour to savor and enjoy.

Parties and dances at night.

The old crowd on the beach daytime.

Get back to it.

That's where you belong, Jonathan.

Back.

Turn back.

Your life will never be the same if you don't.

Never.

Never.

Don't go near that hospital.

Don't go there.

Listen to me, Jonathan.

Please.

Jonathan.

"Jonathan," he whispered to himself.

The man in the next seat suddenly spoke to him. "Going to Seattle or Portland?"

"Seattle," Jonathan said, after a moment's pause.

They were in First Class and the flight attendant had just poured the man's wine. A dark red wine.

Jonathan let his glass of ginger ale stand, untouched. Pale against the dark red.

"Seattle," the man murmured gently and smiled. He raised his glass and sipped the wine with thin, delicate lips. Then he softly set the glass down again. It sparkled in the early afternoon sun, each smooth facet like a cold diamond.

The wine in the glass looked like dark blood to Jonathan. He drove the thought away and listened to the man's low voice.

"I was born there."

"Oh."

"Going to stay with us awhile?" the man asked.

Jonathan shook his head. "Just a day at the most."

The man looked at him curiously and raised the glass again. "A day? That's all?"

"Yes."

The man's eyes were calmly studying Jonathan, as if

he could see into his dark and brooding future. "You'll stay longer," he said.

Jonathan felt a slight tremor go through him.

"How do you know?" he asked.

"You'll stay," the man said.

"I've already booked a flight back. For tomorrow morning," Jonathan said.

The man sipped his wine and then set the glass down again. Firmly.

"You won't get on it," the man said.

The red wine rippled.

Then the man laughed softly and turned to the window and looked out at the massed white clouds.

He didn't speak again to Jonathan the rest of the trip.

Chapter

4

Jonathan phoned Detective Ward, but he was not in his office. He then took a cab to the hospital. He paid the driver, neither saying a word, and then he got out. He stood looking up at the massive gray building. A fine rain was falling from a bleak sky. Evening was coming on, slowly and softly. The leaves of the trees glistened.

He stood on the pavement letting the rain wet his thick, brown, wavy hair. It streaked down onto his tan face, along the small straight nose and then down onto the cleanly defined, determined chin.

He had the Atwood chin, his grandfather would often say admiringly, but not the Atwood eyes. Atwood eyes were blue and almost cold, and they were commanding. Patrician eyes. One of his grandfather's favorite expressions.

"That's what we have. Patrician eyes, Jon."

When an Atwood looks at you with his blue eyes, you know he's looking at you.

"Mine are not blue, Grandfather."

"They're not."

Jonathan's eyes were brown and gentle.

But his body was the Atwood body, tall and muscular. Well-coordinated. With sharp reflexes. Large, strong hands.

"We're a tough breed, Jon."

"I guess we are, Grandfather."

"Nobody fools around with an Atwood."

"Nobody."

His grandfather, still athletic and strong at his advanced age, would pat Jonathan approvingly on the shoulder. "A tough breed. Your brown eyes can flame up at times."

"I guess they can."

"Times you have to fight," Grandfather would say.

"I know."

"And strike down anyone who stands in your way," the old man would add.

"Yes."

"When you take over after me, don't let anyone come in and push you aside. They'll try to do it. They always do."

"I know."

"You remember what I tell you."

Then Peter Atwood would rumple his grandson's hair and a tenderness would come into the commanding voice. "You're the last of the line, Jon. There's nobody left but you and me."

"You're not counting Mother."

And a distant look would come into the old man's eyes. The blue, cool eyes. "I know. She's my only child. My daughter. But she's a Marshall now. Edward Marshall's wife. You're the only one who's going to continue the Atwood name. Always remember that."

"Yes."

"Don't ever let the name die out. Promise me that."

When Jonathan was very young, Peter Atwood had his grandson's name changed to Atwood. Jonathan's father and mother went along with the decision.

I guess he threatened to cut them out of his will, Jonathan thought. In a sense, he bought me. As he's done with everything else he's ever wanted. And he wanted me. Me above all else. He's told me that so many times.

"You're an Atwood," the old man would repeat.

"Yes, Grandfather."

"You're going to have my name. My money. My power. All yours. Yours, Jonathan."

The blue eyes would stare into Jonathan, like points of steel.

"So you watch yourself. You stay away from drugs. And drink. Your mother drinks too much. Too much, Jonathan."

Because she's an unhappy woman, Grandfather. Why? I don't know. I've thought about it many times.

Do you know, Grandfather? She seems to love my father. And he seems to love her. Seems. What do I really know about them? What?

I've lived all my life with you, Grandfather. I see them maybe two or three times a year when they come back to the States. And even then I don't see much of them. And then they're off again. Back to Madrid. Closing all doors behind them. And I'm left standing outside. So cold and alone.

"You keep yourself healthy and alive. Remember that, Jonathan," Grandfather would say.

"I will."

I will, Jonathan thought, and went slowly up the stone steps and into the gray building, feeling all the time that someone under the dark and wet trees was watching him.

Chapter
5

The door to 601 was closed. Jonathan opened it and walked into the silent room. The lone bed was empty. White and neat, as if it had been just newly made.

Jonathan stood there looking at it.

"You came too late," a deep voice said.

Jonathan turned around sharply and looked down into the hazel eyes of a short, stocky man with graying hair. The face was quiet and rugged.

"He's dead," Jonathan said. His voice sounded hollow to him, as if he were standing in an empty room, with shadows on the walls.

"He's dead," the man said.

"When?" Jonathan asked.

"About fifteen minutes ago."

And for some strange, unfathomable reason, Jonathan felt an urge to weep. He turned away from the man and looked out the window and into the darkening sky.

The leaves still glistened in the rain. The dark trunks of the trees were wet and shining under the lamplight.

"I'm Detective Sergeant Ward."

Jonathan turned away from the window. "I phoned you from the airport."

"I was here. He was fading fast. So I came here."

A heavy silence filled the room.

"I told him you were coming. He tried to hold on. But he didn't make it," Ward said.

"He didn't," Jonathan said.

They were silent.

Jonathan kept looking at the white and empty bed.

Trying to imagine the man who once lay upon it. Face agonized and taut, eyes open and desperate.

Desperate to see me, Jonathan thought. Why? Now he can never tell me. Death is so final.

Jonathan stood there in a silence that was deep and pervasive.

From somewhere outside, he heard the distant sound of a church bell. Faint and sad. He wondered if he were imagining it. Then the fragile sound faded into the soft fall of the rain.

He heard the detective's low voice, clear and distinct. "Do you want to go down and take a look at him?"

"Yes."

The man nodded. "Okay," he said. "Let's go."

Jonathan followed him out of the empty room, down the gleaming corridor and then to the closed elevator doors.

They stood there waiting.

The detective spoke. "Ever see a dead person before?"

"No."

"They're the same as live ones. Only they sleep better."

There was a hint of a sardonic smile in the man's eyes.

Jonathan didn't say anything.

The doors opened and they went into the elevator. No one else was in it. Jonathan leaned back against one of the chrome walls. He suddenly felt tired. Tired and drained. His eyes closed and then slowly opened again.

Ward glanced quietly over to him. "How was your trip?" he asked.

"All right," Jonathan said.

"Sleep much?"

"No. I didn't sleep at all."

"Too much on your mind?" Ward asked.

"I guess so."

"Any trouble getting a flight on such short notice?"

Jonathan shook his head. "None."

Ward smiled. "I thought you wouldn't have."

"Why?"

"Your grandfather is on the board of directors of three major airlines."

Jonathan looked at him. "You know that?"

"It's my business to know that," Ward said.

Jonathan didn't speak.

"I've been trying to learn everything I could about you," Ward said.

"About me?"

"A man's been killed. I've been trying to find a connection."

"And?"

"I'm up against a blank wall."

"He told you nothing about himself?" Jonathan asked.

Ward shook his head. "Nothing."

"And you're counting on me?"

"That's right."

The doors opened and nobody came in. The doors shut and they were alone again.

It's as if the detective ordered this elevator for his own private use, Jonathan thought grimly. To grill me.

Then he heard the man speak again. "You seem pretty shaken by all this."

"Maybe I am."

"Why?"

Jonathan didn't answer him.

The detective waited awhile and then softly asked the question again. "Why, Mr. Atwood?"

But before Jonathan could answer, the doors opened and they went out of the elevator.

They walked down a silent corridor. Two doctors in green gowns passed by them, talking quietly. Jonathan noticed blood on one of the gowns. Bright and red. Then the doctors in their gowns turned a corner of the corridor and were gone. Their quiet voices were stilled, lost in the silence that drifted in again, a silence that became close and oppressive.

The detective's voice cut into the silence like a blade. "You didn't answer my question," Ward said.

Jonathan looked at him but didn't speak.

"Well, Mr. Atwood?"

"Why am I so shaken?" Jonathan said.

"Yes."

18

"He's a human being and I feel for him."

The detective shook his head. "No. It's not that at all."

"What is it then?" Jonathan asked.

"You tell me."

"I don't know what you're driving at."

"You do."

"Listen," Jonathan said slowly and evenly. "I can't answer you because there is no answer. I don't know why I feel the way I do about that man."

The detective's hazel eyes were cold and hostile. "You're not keeping something back from me, are you?"

"Why should I?"

"Just answer the question."

"I'm not keeping anything back from you," Jonathan said.

They stopped and stood facing each other.

"That's what you say," Ward said.

"That's exactly what I say."

Ward suddenly turned away from Jonathan. "All right. Let's go in and see if you recognize him."

Ward abruptly pushed open two swinging doors and Jonathan silently followed the detective in. All the time saying to himself: He's right. I am shaken. Deeply shaken. But why? Why?

And then he was standing by the corpse.

Chapter
6

They do sleep better, Jonathan thought sadly. Yes, they do. A long, long sleep. The face was quiet and composed, almost serene. The eyes were blue. Not the Atwood blue. Yet very close to it. The chin was not the Atwood chin. A strong one, but definitely not the Atwood kind.

Jonathan leaned closer to the pale form.

Who was this man? Why did he want to see me? What did he want to ask me? Or tell me?

"You know him?" The detective's hard voice cut through Jonathan's thoughts.

Jonathan didn't answer.

"Well? Tell me."

Jonathan turned away from the dead man and back to Ward.

"I don't," he said.

"What?"

20

And he saw the grim disappointment on the detective's face.

"I tell you I don't know him," Jonathan said.

"Are you sure?"

Jonathan nodded. "Never saw him in my life." Ward's jaw muscles moved, his lips were pressed tightly together, and then he spoke again. "You're not holding back on me, are you?" he asked harshly.

Jonathan's brown eyes flashed. "What did you say?"

"Maybe lying?"

Jonathan stared fiercely at the man. But he didn't speak.

"Answer me," the detective said grimly.

"Why should I lie to you?"

"That's what I'm trying to find out."

Jonathan's voice rose just a bit when he spoke. "I told you I never saw this man before in all my life. That should be more than enough for you."

"Then how did he know so much about you and your family?"

"How?"

"He even knew your private phone number," Ward said.

"That's as much a puzzle to me as it is to you."

"Is it?"

"Yes," Jonathan insisted.

"He was even certain that you would come out here."

Jonathan shook his head. "I don't know how he could have been."

"You did come here, didn't you?"

"I did."

"You could have just as well hung up on me," Ward said.

I could have, Jonathan thought.

The corpse lay silent between them, its blue eyes cold and staring.

Then Jonathan heard the detective's hard police voice again. "He never worked for your grandfather?"

Jonathan shook his head. "No."

"Are you sure?"

"Of course I am," Jonathan said.

The attendant stood in the background, impassively watching the two of them.

"How about in your homes? You have quite a few of them," Ward said.

"We have."

"Well?"

"No."

"Are you sure?" Ward said.

"I never saw him."

"Maybe downtown Manhattan? In the Atwood Building?"

Jonathan looked at him. "Are you serious?"

"Of course I am. Well?"

"The Atwood Building is fifty stories tall," Jonathan said quietly. "There are hundreds and hundreds of people on my grandfather's staff."

"So?"

"So it's virtually impossible to know them all. Even a small percentage of them. For a sergeant of detectives you're asking a very foolish question."

Ward's face paled with anger. "And you're giving me a very arrogant and insulting answer."

"You asked for it," Jonathan said.

"Did I?"

"Yes."

The detective's voice rose when he spoke again. "And I'm only trying to do my job. My job. Something you couldn't understand. Because you're a rich, spoiled brat."

"Am I?" Jonathan asked.

"In spades."

Then Ward suddenly leaned forward and pulled the sheet from the body of the dead man. "Look," he said. He pointed grimly. "Look. This man was beaten to death. Beaten savagely. Look and then come up with your smart-ass answers."

Jonathan trembled and didn't speak. The sight of the bruised, broken body reached into his very soul. He looked and then trembled again. He had to turn away.

The attendant came over and straightened the sheet over the corpse and then moved back into the shadows again.

"All right," Ward said. "Let's get out of here. You're starting to get white around the gills. You'll keel over on me."

"I'm okay," Jonathan said.

"Sure. Come on."

Jonathan followed him out of the large, white-walled room.

His face was pale and moist. He felt weak and slightly nauseous.

"Lean against the wall," Ward said gruffly.

Jonathan leaned back against the wall and looked down at the detective. "I'm sorry," he murmured.

"Just take a few deep breaths."

"Okay."

The two were silent.

Jonathan thought of the bruised, broken body of the dead man and of the two staring blue eyes. Staring into a limitless eternity. He could not forget the eyes. They will always be with me, he thought.

Then he heard the detective's voice. It was gentle now. "Starting to feel better?"

Jonathan nodded. "Yes."

"No longer woozy?"

"Uh-huh."

"You're starting to get back some of your color."

"I feel okay."

"Good."

But the man kept studying him. "I'm sorry I was hard on you," he said.

"That's all right."

"But you are a brat."

"I guess I am." He smiled weakly at the man.

"I've got a son your age," Ward said. "And he's a brat, too."

"But not a rich and spoiled one," Jonathan said.

"He's not rich and I don't make enough to spoil him," Ward smiled. A sad, haunted look came over the rugged face.

When the man spoke again, his voice was low and distant. "We're close, very close. I even discuss my cases with him. He's got a fine, inquisitive mind. And a retentive one. Remembers everything I tell him. Everything. Every little detail of a case. Yes, we're close. And yet there are times when I feel I know as little about him as I do about you. It worries me to my bones. Makes me almost shiver. You're a hard generation to read."

"I guess we are," Jonathan murmured.

"Let's get outside into the air."

Jonathan silently followed him out.

The eyes of the dead man still before him.

Chapter

7

They stood at the head of the stone steps, under a broad wooden covering, watching the rain fall gently before them.

"You seem okay to me now," Ward said.

"I am," Jonathan said.

The detective glanced away from him and out to the soft rain. His rugged face became thoughtful and somber. "I've had people pass out on me. Lots of them. Strong-looking hombres. Even a football player. An all-pro linebacker. The lights go out in their eyes and they're lying on the floor right before me."

He didn't speak for a while. Then he turned back to Jonathan. "Don't let any cop fool you," he said in a quiet voice. "Dead men get to you one way or another. No matter how many you see. But they get to you. When they stop doing that, then you're in trouble. Then it's time to see the department psychiatrist."

Jonathan looked gratefully at him. "Thanks for saying that. I was feeling very—" And he didn't go on.

"Ashamed?"

Jonathan nodded silently.

Ward smiled. "Don't. You did very well in there."

A man walked by them and into the building.

"It was terrible looking at him," Jonathan suddenly said in a low voice. "At what they did to him."

" 'They'?"

"Yes."

"We don't know if it was one person or more than one."

"You have any clues?"

Ward shook his head. "None to work with. All we know is that he was walking in the park just before nightfall, and then it happened."

"And then it happened," Jonathan murmured.

The detective's large hand moved up and down in a harsh gesture. "Quick and brutal. Final. No witnesses. Nothing."

A bitter look came into Jonathan's eyes. "Nothing but a man lying there. Beaten to death."

"Just about. He had no chance. When they brought him into the hospital, he was on his way out. He lasted the way he did from sheer will. That's what I think. He wanted to last."

"Yes," Jonathan whispered.

They stood there gazing into the slowly darkening night. A car swished by on the rainy street below them, and Jonathan watched the red glowing tail lights vanish, and then the street was quiet again. His heart was heavy within him.

27

The detective spoke. "I just can't understand why he wouldn't give me his name. I tried everything but I got nowhere with him."

"No identification?"

"None. The wallet was gone. His pockets were emptied. Not even a penny in them. Nobody reported him missing. Nothing to go on."

Another car swished by. And the street was empty and alone again.

"He was waiting for you," Ward said.

"Yes," Jonathan murmured. "For me."

"And after a while, I was waiting. Just as desperately," Ward said.

"I came here with nothing to give you."

"You came too late. Fifteen minutes too late."

Jonathan winced. "I'm sorry," he said. "Sorry it turned out this way."

Ward shrugged silently.

A woman came out of the building, walked slowly down the wet steps, holding her umbrella over her. Then she turned and disappeared under the wet, shiny leaves of the trees.

"Fifteen minutes," Jonathan said. "My cab was caught in traffic."

The detective was silent, looking out at the rain.

"It all would've been different. He would have spoken to me."

"Yes."

"I wonder what he would have said."

The detective turned coldly away from the rain and looked at Jonathan. "You never saw him before?"

"You already asked me that."

"I know, But I'm asking you again."

Jonathan shook his head grimly. "Never."

They didn't speak.

Finally, the detective glanced at his watch and then turned to Jonathan. "Well, I guess I'll be going now," he said.

"Do you think you'll be needing me anymore?" Jonathan asked.

Ward shook his head. "No. But if I do I'll get in touch with you."

"I'm at the Hotel Meridian."

"When are you leaving?" Ward asked.

"In the morning. Flight 807. Eastern."

"Okay. And thanks for coming out here. It was very decent of you to take the long trip."

He shook Jonathan's hand and then walked down the steps and into the rainy darkness.

Chapter

He was sitting in his hotel room, looking through the glimmering window at the night sky, when the phone rang. The rain had stopped and the moon was coming out from under the cover of the heavy clouds with a bright, silvery shine.

Jonathan picked up the phone.

"Yes?"

There was no answer.

"Hello?"

Still a silence.

Someone was on the other end of the line. He was sure of it. And then he heard. "Jonathan Atwood?" A low, hard voice.

"Speaking."

A man's voice.

Again a pause of silence.

This time he waited without speaking.

And then he heard. "This is a friend."

"Who are you?" Jonathan said.

"With some friendly advice."

Again the pause.

And then the voice again.

"Go back home."

"What?"

"Get on that plane and stay on it."

"Who are you?"

"I told you, a friend."

And then, before Jonathan could speak, he heard the hard, flat voice again. "If you don't make that plane, you'll die. Just like the man in the park did. He wasn't a pretty sight, was he? Remember what I say. Sooner or later. But you'll die."

A sharp click. And the voice was gone. Jonathan slowly put the receiver down.

The cold silver of the moon crept silently into the room.

Ever so silently.

Chapter
9

It was very late when the detective called.

"Just got your message, Jonathan. I was out most of the night."

Jonathan hesitated and then spoke. "I had a strange phone call, Mr. Ward."

"Call me Tom. What was strange about it?"

"A man told me not to stay here in Seattle. To get on the plane and make sure that I went back home."

"Or?"

"I would die."

"You say it was a man?" the detective asked.

"Yes."

"No doubt about the voice?"

"None. It was a man."

There was a long pause.

"Tom?" Jonathan finally said.

"I'm here. Just thinking."

"He also told me I'd die like the man in the park did," Jonathan said.

"If you stay here."

"Yes."

Again the silence. Then he heard. "Anything else?"

"That was all he said."

"I see."

"Just that he was a friend giving me some friendly advice," Jonathan said.

"Very friendly." The detective's voice was sardonic. Jonathan could almost see a grim smile on the rugged face.

"Just thought you should know about the call," Jonathan said.

"Sure. You did right to contact me."

"What do you make of it, Tom?"

And he thought he could hear the man sigh. "I don't know, Jonathan. But I do know this. You get on that plane and you go on home. Do as you were told. I'll take it from here."

"All right," Jonathan said.

"I woke you up, didn't I?"

"Not really. I was in bed but I . . ." He didn't go on.

"You weren't able to sleep," Ward said gently. "The call upset you."

"It shook me up."

"Of course."

"And it angered me," Jonathan said.

"Oh?"

"Frightened and angered me."

"I see."

33

Jonathan's voice became tight. "Who does he think he is, anyway? Telling me what to do."

"Jonathan."

"Yes."

"Who does he think he is? A murderer. That's what he is. And he can murder again. Very easily."

Jonathan was silent.

"So you control your anger and your fear. Try and get some sleep. I know you won't. But try anyway. Okay?" Tom said.

"Okay," Jonathan murmured.

"And get on that plane."

"I will."

"That's better. Good-bye, lad."

"Good-bye, Tom."

Jonathan put out the lights and got back into bed.

The darkness of the night covered him with a cold, deep silence.

Chapter
10

He had called Walter the night before to let him know of his flight back home and to have the black limousine pick him up at Kennedy Airport.

Now it was morning.

He was sitting in one of the many small waiting rooms at the Seattle airport, waiting for the boarding time of his plane to be announced.

He tried to read the morning newspaper. But it was no use. The words had no meaning to him. None at all.

Jonathan folded the newspaper carefully and set it down by his side. He took off his shell-rimmed glasses, put them back into their case, and then put the case into his inside pocket with slow, measured motions. But his hand trembled, ever so slightly.

He was about to get up and start walking about the waiting room just to release the tension inside him, when someone noiselessly slid into the empty seat next to him.

Then he heard the voice. "You're Jonathan Atwood, aren't you?"

It was a girl's voice. Low and soft and modulated. A voice he never again forgot. Never.

Jonathan turned. "Yes. I am," he said.

"I thought so. Could we talk?" the girl said.

"About what?"

"I'm Jenny Mason."

"Am I supposed to know you?"

The girl shook her head and her thick, auburn hair swirled and caught the glints of morning sun coming through the airport windows. "No, I'm just telling you my name."

She was about his age, tall and slim and attractive.

Jenny Mason.

A name he never would forget.

Never.

She wore a white sweater and a checkered skirt. The University of Washington logo was stitched on the front of her sweater. About her neck was a loosely tied silk scarf. Pink.

"I see you're flying back to New York," she said.

"I am."

"To Southhampton."

Jonathan looked coldly into her clear, gray eyes. "How do you know I live in Southhampton?"

She didn't answer.

"How?" he asked again.

When she spoke, her voice was very quiet and low.

But each word was clear and distinct. "Because the man who was killed told me."

Jonathan paled. "What?"

"He carried a photograph of you in his wallet."

"Of me?"

"Yes," she said.

"Why?"

She didn't answer.

He suddenly gripped her arm and asked again fiercely. "Why? Tell me."

"Let me go."

"Tell me," he insisted.

She pulled away from his grasp and as she did, the pink scarf slid, and he saw a long, disfiguring scar on her white neck.

A hurt, defensive look came into her gray eyes.

He felt as though he had uncovered her, and a pang went through him.

He saw her hand go to the scarf and settle it once more into place and then tie the knot tighter.

They sat in silence.

Then he heard her speak again.

"He never told me why," she said.

Jonathan turned and gazed silently at her.

"You must believe me. I don't know why he carried your photograph," Jenny said.

"And you never asked?" he said gently.

She shook her head.

Jonathan hesitated before he spoke "Who was he?"

"His name was Alfred Kaplan."

"Kaplan?"

"Yes."

"I never heard the name mentioned. Never in my life."

He looked away from her attractive face and out through the windows at the silver planes and the clear bright sky overhead.

Then her voice came through to him. "He taught English at the University. Taught it for many years."

Jonathan still gazed at the vast, limitless sky and waited for her to speak again.

"I was one of his students. That's how I got to know him," Jenny said.

"What sort of a man was he?"

"Kept to himself. Lived by himself."

"A loner," Jonathan said.

"Yes. But in class an excellent and devoted teacher. Everyone was his friend. But once out of his class he closed up."

"And became a loner again."

"Yes."

Yet you became his friend, Jonathan thought. "Did he have a wife? Children?" he asked.

She shook her head. "No. He once told me he never married."

"I saw him in the hospital morgue. He was a handsome man."

"He was," she said softly.

"Even in death. Was he gay?"

She looked directly at him. "Why do you ask that?"

He shrugged. "Just asked."

"No," she said coldly. "He was not gay." And then he heard her say, "It's always the gentle and the good people of this world who are killed. Isn't that so?"

38

He turned back to her. "I don't know," he said.

A harsh, bitter look came into her eyes. "It is so. The gentle and the good are always hurt and cut and destroyed. It's always been that way. Always."

He thought of the jagged scar on her neck and didn't say anything.

And then he heard her speak again, in her low, modulated voice. "Don't get on that plane."

He stared silently at her.

"I want you to help me find his murderers," she said.

"What?"

"We can do it. If you'll stay here with me."

"Stay? In Seattle?" Jonathan asked.

"Yes."

He shook his head. "That's impossible."

"It isn't."

"I'm going back home. There's no reason for me to stay here anymore."

She put her hand on his and its warmth coursed through him. "Don't go, Jonathan. You owe it to him to stay here."

"What do you mean?" he asked.

She didn't answer.

"What are you holding back from me? What is it that you know?"

Suddenly they heard the boarding announcement. The voice of the loudspeaker cut through them like a sharp sword.

Jonathan rose.

Jenny rose, too, tall and straight. "Don't take that plane. Or you'll regret it for the rest of your life."

39

They heard the announcement again.

"You will," she said.

He didn't speak.

He stood there hesitant, looking into her clear, gray eyes. Listening to her voice.

"Come with me," she said. "I'll take you to the house he lived in. See it. Look around it. I'll answer your questions there. And then you can make up your mind. You can always take a later plane if you wish. You know you can."

Her voice stopped.

A strange silence seemed to fill the boarding lounge. He saw the people of First Class beginning to board the plane. One by one. Time seemed to stand still. The passengers seemed to walk in slow motion.

"Stay," she said.

"No."

Her voice became desperate. "Do you believe in fate? Fate brought us together. It did."

"I'm going," he said.

"Jonathan."

He couldn't look into her pleading eyes anymore. "No," he said.

He turned abruptly and walked away from her but her voice made him stop and face her.

She came to him. "Jonathan," she said. "Please listen to me. Please."

"Listen to you?" he said desperately. "I don't even know who you are."

"True."

Her clean fragrance surrounded him.

"I don't even know who he was," he said.

"Stay and find out."

"Why haven't you gone to the police? They've been trying to find out who he is. You can tell them," Jonathan said.

"Why?"

"Yes. Why?" he repeated.

"I have a reason. A good reason," Jenny said.

"What is it?"

"Just come with me. Trust me."

He stood there looking at the pink scarf and listening to her voice.

"Trust me, Jonathan."

She was close to him.

Who are you? he said to himself. Who? That I should trust you.

But he heard himself say, in a voice that was distant and strange to him, "I'll take a later plane."

He thought he saw tears come to her eyes, but he couldn't be sure because she quickly turned away from him and started walking toward the exit.

He followed her out of the airport to her car.

Chapter

11

Two tall, stocky figures in black leather boots, camouflage khaki fatigues, got up from their seats at the end of the airport waiting room and went outside.

Their heads, shaved bald, glinted in the sun.

"What do you think, Carl?"

Carl stood watching Jonathan and the girl get into a car. His icy blue eyes hardened. "He didn't take my advice, Mitch," he said. He was in his early twenties, but his voice was hard and flat. His lips were thin and bloodless.

"Didn't get on that plane," Mitch said.

"No." Carl's big hand tightened into a fist and then slowly relaxed. There was a small Nazi swastika tattooed on his tanned wrist. "That plane is gone now."

"It sure is," Mitch said. He was Carl's age. A red bandana was tied around his thick neck. He now raised it and secured it around his head, like a sweatband.

"There'll be other planes," Carl said.

"I know."

They were silent as they watched the car slowly make its way out of the parking lot.

Mitch stroked the stubble of beard on his broad, heavy face. "I don't like this," he said in a low voice.

"Why?"

"It's dangerous to have him around."

Carl didn't speak.

"There's some connection between him and Kaplan. I got a gut feeling about that. And it's not a good one," Mitch said.

"So?"

"His grandfather is a very rich and very powerful man. Could be trouble."

"We'll be able to handle it," Carl said.

"But if he gets close?"

"He won't. Listen. Kaplan died without saying a word to anybody. Not to Atwood. And not to the detective," Carl said. He lit a cigarette and threw away the burnt matchstick with an abrupt and harsh gesture. "Get close? What do Skinheads do when you crowd them?"

They looked quietly at each other.

Mitch slowly nodded his head. "Blow him away," he said.

Carl inhaled deeply and then let the smoke out through his thin nostrils. "We're Skinheads. We're in a war. Never forget that."

"I don't," Mitch said.

"He starts anything he's dead meat," Carl said.

"Like Kaplan."

"Like him."

The two stood there motionless, their shaved heads glinting in the sun, their shadows long on the ground.

Chapter
12

Jonathan sat at the girl's side as she drove smoothly up one of the sparkling, wooded hills that overlooked the city. The sun shone in a clear blue sky and the trees were green with flickering leaves. He felt the touch of a soft breeze on his face, cool and soothing.

It's such a beautiful day, he thought wistfully. Rare and beautiful, like the golden days on the Southhampton beaches.

I should be there now, he thought, lying under the glowing sun and hearing the sound of careless laughter. Feeling the joy of being young and alive. Alive.

I look about me now and see this sparkling beauty and yet underneath it all lies the dark threat of death. My death.

Just as underneath the pink silk scarf lies the mark of some savage cruelty. Yes.

Savage? Cruelty? Why do I think that? How do I know how she got that scar? How?

What do I know about her?

Nothing. Absolutely nothing. Who is she?

It was madness to listen to her. Why did I do it? Just because she's so beautiful? Almost breathtaking?

Nonsense. I've been with beautiful girls before. Some even more beautiful than she is. And yet he kept glancing at her clean and attractive profile, at her softly curved lips.

She kept looking at the road, driving with clear, gray, impassive eyes. Never once turning to him. Never once saying a word.

Jenny, he thought. I like the name. I like it very much. It seems to belong to her. It does. I couldn't even think of her with any other name.

Jennifer. It must be that. Jenny.

"Jenny," he said.

She half-turned to him, her auburn hair flashing in the sun. "Yes?"

He kept looking at her. "Nothing," he said.

She turned back to the sunlit highway.

The two were silent again.

He looked at her and thought of his grandfather, Peter Atwood. Tall and stern and patrician.

Grandfather, I want to introduce you to a girl I met out in Seattle.

Yes?

This is Jennifer. Jennifer Mason of the Seattle Masons.

The Seattle Masons, Jonathan?

Isn't she beautiful?

46

She is.

What do you think of her?

And before he could imagine his grandfather's answer, Jonathan realized that the girl had turned the car off the sunlit highway and onto a narrow macadam road that led through high, leafy trees flanking the road like silent sentinels. The houses were spaced farther apart. A car passed by and the road was deserted again. Deserted and solitary. He felt a cold feeling creep over him.

Then he heard her speak. "We're about there now," she said quietly.

"At his place?"

"Yes."

The cold feeling stayed with him.

She slowed the car, turned down a gravel driveway, and there was the dead man's house.

Jenny stopped the car. All was quiet about them. Deadly quiet.

Jonathan thought of the man lying on a slab in the hospital morgue, the blue eyes staring intently into eternity. He heard her low voice.

"Okay?" she asked.

"Yes," he said.

They stepped out of the car, and he heard the sound of the metal doors opening and shutting. The hollow sound clattered against the tall, somber trees and died slowly away. They walked a few steps and then paused under the shade of the trees, the sunlight flickering like little flames between the still leaves, flickering onto the ground beneath, as if trying to set it afire.

In front of him stood a small green and white house

47

with a small front porch. The house was wooden and had two stories. Jonathan gazed up at it and thought of the man sitting on the porch, silent and alone, looking out at the dark circle of trees, sitting there until the dark night came quietly down and covered him, leaving only two sad eyes staring into eternity.

"Jonathan."

He turned to her.

"Let's go in." Jenny said.

"All right." His voice was low and tight.

They went up the wooden steps, onto the porch, and then stopped by the closed door.

He watched Jenny take out a key and then open the door.

He followed her in.

Chapter
13

It was strange. Very strange. But he felt the aura, the presence of the dead man in every neat, little room of the house.

As though Alfred Kaplan were there at his side. Silent. Noiseless. Pale. Very pale. Walking slowly with Jonathan and matching every step that he made. Pausing when Jonathan paused. And then gliding away and standing still in a dim corner, quietly gazing at the younger man, the blue eyes now soft and gentle. And appraising.

It was strange.

He felt that the dead man was there with him, particularly in the study, a small upstairs room that overlooked a back garden.

Jonathan stepped over the threshold of the study and then stopped and looked about him. His eyes rested on the full bookshelves, then moved slowly to the old upright typewriter on the weathered desk, and from there to the delicate paintings on the soft gray walls and the little pieces of exquisite sculpture scattered about with a nice harmony. And as Jonathan stood there in a great and profound silence, he knew why Jenny had wanted him to come to the house.

This was the home of a civilized human being. Civilized and cultivated.

As he stood there, holding one of the pieces of sculpture in his big hand, a chill swept over him. He saw again with horror the detective lifting the white sheet showing him the broken and battered body of Alfred Kaplan. He could almost hear the cries of agony as the man was being savagely beaten.

Jonathan's eyes closed for an instant with pain.

And Jenny's words came back to him with a bitter force.

Why do the good and the gentle suffer so much in this world? Why are they beaten and cut and destroyed? Why, Jonathan?

I don't know, Jenny, he whispered to himself. I just don't know.

His hand touched the typewriter almost tenderly and then fell softly away from it.

Jenny stood behind him, silent and still.

I don't know, Jenny.

His hand clenched and unclenched with despair, bleak, empty despair.

And then there was something else strange. Something he could not explain. And it was this: that somewhere, somewhere in the very dim past he had met this man. Met and talked with him.

And then he said to himself, Never. Couldn't be that. I would remember. Surely remember.

Maybe he had seen the face somewhere?

No.

A photograph.

But where? When?

He saw again the calm face and open blue eyes of the dead man, open and staring.

And then he said to himself fiercely, This is non-sense. Madness.

I've never seen that face anywhere before. Never.

I'm sure of that. Positive. Beyond any doubt.

I've got to stop this and get out of here.

He looked coldly at Jenny and then turned abruptly away from her and went over to an old easy chair and sat down.

What am I doing here? he asked himself. I should go home. Take the next plane out and get away from all this.

I'll have her drive me back to the airport. I'll tell her to do it now. Now.

But he didn't say anything.

He just sat there and gazed through the clear window at the circle of dark trees. He felt caught and hemmed in by those silent trees. Silent and dark. Inscrutable. Like fate.

And he thought of her words to him in the airport.

Fate. Do you believe in fate, Jonathan?

No, Jenny. I don't.

Fate brought us together, Jonathan.

No.

It did. I'm sure of it.

Listen to me, Jenny. Like my grandfather, I believe that you make your own destiny. Forget fate and all that nonsense. I'm doing what he would do. I'm getting up now and taking that plane out of here. I'm going back to Southhampton. To the sun and the beach and the life I've always had. Drive me back, Jenny. Now.

And it was then that he heard her voice, low and modulated. "Don't go back, Jonathan."

He slowly turned to her.

Her face was white and taut.

"Stay here with me," she said.

He trembled but he shook his head firmly. "I'm leaving."

"Listen to me. Please."

"There's nothing to listen to, Jenny."

She came close to him. "There is. Alfred Kaplan was not mugged as the police believe."

"What do you mean?" he asked.

"It was made to look like a mugging."

"And?"

"It wasn't that. Wasn't that at all. He was deliberately murdered."

He stared silently at her.

"I'm telling you the truth, Jonathan," she said. "He was killed by the Skinheads."

"Skinheads?"

"Yes. They are a bunch of cruel, young racists. Cruel and vicious."

"They deliberately killed him?"

"Yes."

"How do you know it?" he asked.

"Because they had good reason to."

"Why?"

"You must believe me," she said.

"I don't have to believe anything," he said coldly.

She stood there looking at him and then without a word she turned and went over to the desk.

He watched her open one of the drawers and take out a sheet of white typing paper.

She came over to him.

And he said to himself, how beautiful you are, Jenny. How very beautiful.

He heard her low voice. "This is the title page of a book he was writing."

She handed him the page and he read it silently.

SKINHEAD
A study of the movement
and its threat to our country
By Alfred Kaplan

"Skinheads," he murmured.

"We have them here in the Seattle area. Like lice."

He didn't speak. He thought of the man lying dead under the white sheet. Then he heard her say in a low bitter voice, "Lice. Most of them shave their heads clean and wear military fatigues. As if they're fighting a war."

"A war?"

"Yes. To save their country from Blacks, Jews, Hispanics, Orientals . . . all those who aren't, in their bigoted eyes, one hundred percent Americans. And who don't think and act as they do."

"They sound like Nazis," Jonathan said.

She nodded and her eyes flashed. "And like them they beat up and kill people who disagree with them."

"So you say the Skinheads killed Alfred Kaplan?"

"Yes," she said.

Jonathan handed the page back to her.

"How did they find out he was doing the book?" he asked.

"I don't know. But they did. They threatened him. But he went on just the same."

"Until they murdered him and stopped the book."

She shook her head. "They didn't stop the book."

"What do you mean?" he asked.

"He finished it two nights before they got to him. He gave it to me to put in a safe deposit box in Seattle."

"And that's where it is now?" he asked.

"Yes."

"You're going to try to have it published?"

"It will be published," she said grimly.

"You'll see to it?"

"Yes. If it's the last thing I do."

"The last thing," he murmured.

He looked away from her pale, taut face to the circle of dark, silent trees. They seemed to have moved closer to him, standing still like a dark, impenetrable wall. He could see nothing beyond them.

Then he heard her low voice. "Will you stay, Jonathan?"

He didn't answer.

"Please help me. There is no one else to turn to," she said.

"What about the police?"

54

Her lips thinned. "They're hostile and useless," she said.

"Why?"

"Just trust me. I know."

He looked down into the gray, pleading eyes. "Trust you?" he asked.

"Please, Jonathan. I'm all alone in this."

He still stood there looking at her. "Why, Jenny?" he suddenly asked. "Why must it be you?"

She wavered. "Why me?"

"Yes."

"Because he was a decent man and they are monsters."

He shook his head. "No. It's something else."

"There isn't, Jonathan. A good and gentle man was savagely murdered. A man I knew well. A man I admired. I consider myself a decent human being. How can I stand by and not do anything? How?"

He shook his head again.

"What else is there, Jenny? Tell me."

"There is no other reason."

His voice became hard. "You're holding back something. I feel that you are."

"Nothing."

"Jenny."

"I tell you there is nothing," she said.

But deep within him he knew that she was lying to him. She was hiding something. There was something else. There was. But he felt she would never tell him.

They stood there in a cold silence.

He studied her face. Her clear gray eyes. The pink scarf. And the jagged scar underneath.

I'm caught up, he said to himself. And there is no way out.

I never should have stepped on that plane to come out here. I never should have listened to that detective in the first place. Never. Never. Never.

I should've jammed the phone down and gone back to sleep. I should . . . have . . .

Then he heard her voice. "Well, Jonathan?"

He drew in his breath. "If I stay then you must do as I tell you," he said.

Her lips trembled. "You'll stay?"

"Yes."

"Jonathan," she said.

"But on one condition."

"What is that?"

"We go to the police. To Detective Ward."

Her eyes darkened. "No."

"We must," he said.

"Jonathan, I tell you it won't be . . ."

He cut her off. "Only on that condition, Jenny."

She didn't speak.

"Jenny?"

Her face paled.

"Toward the end Alfred Kaplan started to distrust the police."

"Why?"

But she didn't answer him. "I've always distrusted them. Always," she said.

"Why, Jenny?"

An intense, almost mad look came into her eyes. "Because some Skinheads have infiltrated them."

"That's nonsense, Jenny."

56

"But—"

"Enough," he cut in sharply. "We're going to wait here until it is dark. And then we're going back to Seattle."

She slowly, silently nodded.

Chapter

14

There was no moon out and the road was dark.

He drove the car between the two rows of tall, motionless trees with Jenny at his side.

Neither spoke.

The silence was vast and wide around them. The only sound was that of the tires on the surface of the macadam road. Smooth and hushed.

He glanced at her white, tense face, her large gray eyes staring into the deep, impenetrable night. He saw her lips quiver. She seemed so vulnerable to him at that instant. So fragile, so lost.

Jenny, he whispered to himself.

He wanted to reach out his big right hand and put it on hers. Warmly, tenderly. Just to tell her that he was with her. All the way. That he would stay with her until it was all over. Until the killers were caught and taken care of. Until the book was accepted for publication.

I'll help you do it, Jenny, he said to himself. I will. I've made my decision. I'll help you pay your debt to Alfred Kaplan. Whatever it is. I'll do it. Jenny, I'm going to tell you all this now. Now. But he said nothing and did not move his hand from the steering wheel.

He drove on.

Into the night.

Chapter

15

A few miles before he reached the turnoff, Jonathan suddenly sensed that a car had pulled out from a driveway and had begun to follow him.

His heart quickened its beat.

He kept glancing up at the mirror at the cold, glaring headlights behind him.

He was sure that Jenny was aware of them, too. But she never turned her head to look back. Never said a word to him. Just sat there staring ahead of her.

Jonathan speeded up his car just a bit, and then he noticed that the cream-colored car behind him did the same.

He slowed down and the car drew closer to him. He could now make out the dark forms of two men sitting in the front, straight and motionless, their eyes piercing into the darkness. It seemed to him that he could make out the gleam of their heads. Their bald, cleanly-shaven heads.

A chill came over him.

Skinheads? Could it be possible?

His hands tightened over the steering wheel. His lips became a thin, hard line.

Skinheads.

But when he left the road to merge with the highway traffic going to Seattle, he saw that he had been wrong. The cream-colored car kept going down the macadam road until its glowing red taillights disappeared into the darkness.

He breathed a low sigh of relief.

You were wrong, he said to himself. Dead wrong. Stop seeing ghosts where there are none.

He settled back in his seat and drove on.

He felt good having her at his side, close to him. As though he had known her a long, long time. It was a good feeling.

"The car that followed us," Jenny suddenly said.

He turned to her.

"It had Skinheads in it," she said.

The warm feeling dissolved. A chill took its place. His hand tightened over the steering wheel.

"You're sure?" he asked.

"Yes."

He waited for her to say more. But she looked away from him and out to the highway and was silent.

He drove along until he saw a phone booth, and he pulled over onto the shoulder of the highway and got out of the car.

She looked at him.

61

"I'm calling Tom Ward," he said to her.

"The detective?"

"Yes."

He dialed Ward's number and waited. After the third ring, there was a click and a voice said, "Yes?" It was a young man's voice. About his age.

"Detective Ward?"

"No. This is his son, Jed. Who wants him?"

"Jonathan Atwood."

"Does he know you?" His voice sounded hard, cold.

"Yes. Is he there?" Jonathan asked.

"Is it important?"

"Very. I'd like to come and talk to him."

"Where are you now?"

"On Thirty-eight East. Just below Belleville," Jonathan said.

"That's about an hour from here. We're going to a game together about that time."

"Could I please speak to him?"

"You're near Belleville?" Jed asked.

"That's right," Jonathan said.

And he wondered about the question later on. Much later on it became clear to him. Tragically clear.

"I'll get him. What's the name again?" Jed asked.

"Jonathan Atwood."

He waited and looked over to Jenny. Her head was bent low, away from him. He wanted to drop the receiver and go over to her.

"Jonathan?"

He recognized the crisp tone of Ward's voice.

He turned away from Jenny and spoke into the phone. "Yes," he said.

"Where are you?"

"Still in Seattle."

"What's the matter?" Ward asked.

"I've got to see you tonight."

"Why?"

"I'll tell you when I see you."

"No. Tell me now," Ward said.

"I can be at your house in an hour."

The detective's voice became harsh. "I said, tell me now."

"I know who the dead man is. His name is Alfred Kaplan."

"Kaplan?"

"Yes," Jonathan said.

"What else do you know?" Ward asked.

"He was a professor of literature at the University."

"Uh-huh."

"He was killed by the Skinheads," Jonathan said.

"The Skinheads?"

"Yes."

There was a pause.

"Detective Ward?"

"I'm here. How do you know he was killed by them? You have proof?"

"It wasn't a mugging. It was a deliberate and planned killing."

Again the pause. He waited. And then he heard, "I ask you again, how do you know it was the Skinheads?"

"I have no real proof. But I . . ."

He heard the man sigh. "All right. You'll tell me when you get here."

Jonathan didn't say a word about Jenny. Later on, when he thought it over, he wondered why. He could have mentioned her. But he didn't.

He heard the man's voice again. "You know my address?"

"Yes."

"Give it to me," Ward said.

"Fourteen Eustace Lane."

"I thought so. It's twenty-four."

"That's what they gave me at police headquarters," Jonathan said.

"They're always getting it wrong. Where are you now?"

"On Thirty-eight East. Just below Belleville."

"Okay. Go down Highland and turn off there. After three miles or so make a right on Eustace. A small dead end street. I live near the end of the block."

"Highland into Eustace," Jonathan repeated.

"That's it. I'll be waiting for you."

"Good-bye."

"Good-bye, Jonathan. And take care."

"I will."

But there was no click.

Instead Jonathan heard the man speak again. "Just a moment."

There was a pause and then he came back on. "My son reminds me that we have tickets for a baseball game. You'd better be here in an hour. If you're not, you'll have to reach me some time tomorrow at the office."

"I'll be there on time."

"Okay."

When he got back to the car, he saw tears in Jenny's eyes.

"What is it, Jenny?"

She shook her head and turned away from him.

"Jenny."

But she wouldn't tell him.

Chapter
16

Jonathan turned the corner and drove slowly down the quiet, tree-lined street, looking for the number of the detective's house. He found it and then moved in front of a black station wagon and started to park. The station wagon was empty.

The street was silent and deserted. Shining pools of lamplight with stark darkness between them. The white and gray stucco houses stood apart from each other with wide, smooth lawns separating them. There were lights in some of the front windows, but the shades were down and the blinds drawn against the night.

At the end of the narrow street was a small, fenced-in park with benches and a tiny playground. The children were home, quiet and dreaming in their beds. A forgotten toy lay by a gray sandbox. The swings were ghostly and still.

Off in the distance Jonathan heard the desolate cry of

a boat whistle out on Puget Sound. It faded away. He shut the motor off. And now all was vast and silent about him.

He thought of Alfred Kaplan, and of the detective ripping aside the white sheet to reveal the man's broken and bruised body. He felt again the horror within him, the horror and the pity.

And it was then that he heard the low, hard voice. "Get out of the car."

He turned and saw a gun pointed at his head and then above its glinting barrel, the cold eyes of the man.

He heard Jenny's low gasp of terror. He felt her move closer to him. Her hand gripped his arm.

"What do you want?" Jonathan asked fiercely.

The lamplight shone on the bald head and the tight face of the man. "I told you. Get out of the car."

He wore a camouflage jacket and pants. His black combat boots gleamed.

He pointed his gun at Jenny. "You stay put," he said.

Jonathan slowly opened the door and got out of the car.

"What do you want with him?" Jenny asked.

The man motioned curtly with his left hand.

Jonathan saw a small swastika tattooed on his thick wrist.

"You just drive away and get lost."

"Let him alone," Jenny said.

The man's eyes narrowed. "You heard what I said. If you go to the police, he's dead meat. You got that?"

She didn't speak.

"I said, did you get it?"

"Yes," she murmured.

Jonathan stood there and saw the lost, pleading look in Jenny's eyes. He felt a dull, aching anger within him. Aching and hopeless.

He heard the low, hard voice again. The man was speaking to Jenny. She had moved over to the driver's seat.

"We'll kill him," the man said. "You make the wrong move. You know we can do it."

"Yes," she whispered. "I know."

"Get going. Fast now."

She looked one lingering last time at Jonathan. He wondered if he would ever see her again. He wanted to cry out to her. Jenny! But her eyes were now turned away from him.

Then he watched the car drive off into the bleak night.

She was gone.

He was alone now. Utterly alone. And a great, despairing emptiness came over him. Jenny, Jenny, don't leave me. He pressed his lips tight together.

And then he heard. "Walk. Ahead of me."

Jonathan felt the gun barrel hard in his back. He silently nodded.

"Don't try anything stupid."

"I won't," Jonathan muttered.

As he walked past the detective's house, he glanced longingly at the closed door, hoping against hope that it would fling open and Tom Ward would come rushing out, gun in hand.

But no door opened.

And no detective appeared.

Chapter
17

He saw, parked under the thick, leafy branches of a large oak tree, the cream-colored car. It gleamed dully in the darkness.

A man stood by the open doors of the car. He was tall and stocky and he wore a camouflage jacket and pants. His boots were black. A red bandana was tied around his bald head. His eyes glistened when he saw Jonathan, glistened with cruel satisfaction.

"I see you got him, Carl."

"No sweat, Mitch."

He turned to Jonathan. "Get in."

Jonathan stood there hesitant.

"You heard me, didn't you?"

Jonathan didn't move. A mad impulse came to him. What if I shoved him aside and made a run for it? Into the darkness.

He was about to follow that impulse when he felt the

barrel of the gun hit his face and scrape down across his lips. He staggered.

Carl shoved him into the back of the car and then moved in beside him. "When I tell you to do something, you do it," he said.

Jonathan put his hand to his lips and felt the dripping blood.

Carl reached over and shut the door.

"You remember that," he said grimly.

I'll remember, Jonathan thought fiercely.

He reached into his pocket.

Carl leaned toward him. "What are you doing?" he asked.

"Getting a handkerchief."

"All right. But watch yourself. No tricks."

Jonathan drew out the handkerchief and pressed it to his lips. He felt the tenderness and the pain.

You bet I'll remember, he said to himself. My time will come. It has to, Skinhead. Then I'll let you have it. In spades.

"Any trouble with him, Carl?"

"None, Mitch."

"The kooky girl?"

"She' gone. Let's get out of here," Carl said.

"Okay."

Mitch slammed the front door shut and started up the motor.

Carl turned and looked coldly at Jonathan. "Still bleeding?" he asked.

Jonathan didn't answer.

"I told you not to do anything stupid. And you were going to, weren't you?"

"Maybe."

Carl grinned. "Maybe. Got you nothing but blood."

Jonathan stared through the window at the dark night. The car sped along the silent streets and then turned onto the highway. Jonathan thought of Jenny. He saw again her large, terrified eyes before she had turned away from him.

And then he heard Carl's low, hard voice. "I told you to take the plane out of here. Why didn't you?"

"Because he had to listen to the kook," Mitch said.

"Yeah."

"She's bad news, Jonathan," Mitch called out.

Carl nodded and grinned. "That's right. Didn't your daddy teach you that all women are bad news, Jonny Boy?"

"Didn't he, Jonny Boy?" Mitch repeated.

"Bad, bad news," Carl said.

The two began to laugh.

Jonathan's hands clenched into two large fists and then slowly unclenched. My time will come, he thought grimly.

As the car passed under a lamplight he saw the blood on his handkerchief. His eyes glinted. It will come, you Skinheads. It will. Suddenly Mitch began to sing, in a low, whining voice:

> Alfred Kaplan was a Jew
> And a Jew is a Kike
> And what is there to like
> In a Jew Kike?

"What is there?" Carl asked Jonathan.

"Tell him," Mitch called out.

71

"Tell me, Jonny Boy."

"Lay off," Jonathan said.

Carl grinned. "Did you hear him?"

"I heard him," Mitch said, and started singing again. This time he used other words to the tune.

> Blacks
> Blacks
> Blacks
> They call them Blacks now
> How nice
> How cute
> They call them Blacks now
> Blacks
> Blacks
> Blacks
> But where do they come from?
> Where?

He suddenly stopped singing and Carl turned to Jonathan.

"Where do they come from?" he asked.

"Tell him," Mitch said.

"Tell me, Jonny Boy," Carl said, and laughed as he saw the flame in Jonathan's eyes. "Go on, Mitch."

Mitch began to sing again:

> They come from the jungle
> The jungle
> The jungle
> The jungle.

"And where are they going back?" Carl sang.
"To the jungle," Mitch answered.
"To the jungle."
The two sang in harsh harmony.

> We're sending them back to the jungle
> The jungle
> The jungle
> The jungle

Jonathan bowed his head and tried not to listen.

> The jungle
> The jungle

Finally, the two stopped singing.
And silence flowed back into the dark car.
A long silence.

Chapter
18

As they rode through the night, Jonathan found himself thinking again of Alfred Kaplan, searching his memory, trying to discover if he had ever seen or met the man before. But it was no use. He had no recollection of him.

He wondered why Kaplan had wanted so desperately to see him and to talk to him. What did Kaplan want to tell him?

What has he to do with my life? Or it could be with my death? There must be some connection. Somewhere.

Does Jenny know and is not telling me? But what would be her reason?

Jenny. Why do they call her a kook? Why? These men are animals. Not human beings.

And then he heard Mitch speak in a low voice to Carl. "We're coming to the border."

"Okay. Give me your bandana."

"What do you want it for?" Mitch asked.

"Just hand it over and shut up."

"Carl, don't try any more rough stuff with him. Not yet."

"I'm not. Give it to me."

Jonathan saw Mitch reluctantly take the bandana from around his bald head and hand it to Carl. He waited with growing anxiety.

"Put your head down," Carl said to Jonathan.

"What?"

"Do as I tell you," Carl ordered.

"Do it, Jonny Boy. He's got a short fuse," Mitch said.

Jonathan bowed his head, and then he felt Carl tie the bandana over his eyes.

"Can you see anything?" Carl asked.

"No."

"That's how I want it."

"Now you don't know where we're taking you. Do you, Jonny Boy?" Mitch called out.

"Just cool it, Mitch."

"Okay."

"You talk too much," Carl said harshly. He turned to Jonathan. "You can straighten up now."

Jonathan slowly sat up again.

Then he heard Carl's mocking voice. "Relax and enjoy the ride."

"That's it, Jonny Boy. Relax," Mitch said.

The two began to laugh. And then they were silent again. Two dark, motionless figures.

After a while, Jonathan felt the car leave the smooth

surface of the highway and move along the ruts of a dirt road.

He felt with his fingers along his lips.

The bleeding had stopped.

His fingers were dry.

He closed them into a fist.

Chapter
19

He felt the bandana being taken off his eyes.

The car had stopped.

He opened his eyes and saw the moon riding high in a dark sky, bright and gleaming. He put his hand up to shade them from the light and then he heard Carl's voice.

"Get out and no tricks," Carl said.

He put his gun up to Jonathan's face, the barrel softly scraping his cheek.

"Okay?"

Jonathan didn't speak.

"Answer me," Carl said.

"Okay," Jonathan muttered.

He stepped out of the car and looked around. Straight ahead was a large wooden farmhouse, its windows un-lit. To the right as a barn and beyond that a stretch of field. In the distance was the glittering outline of a mountain range. The air was soft and chilling.

"Take him to the barn and lock him in," Carl ordered.

Mitch took out his gun and pointed it at Jonathan.

"We'll talk to you in the morning," Carl said.

"About what?" Jonathan asked.

"About whether we should kill you or not," Carl said.

"How's that for starters?" Mitch asked.

The two began to laugh.

"Get moving," Mitch said.

Jonathan walked slowly along the grassy path to the dark barn, the man close behind him.

Jonathan looked past the bleak form of the barn to the sharp outlines of the mountains glittering in the moonlight. He felt a sudden yearning sweep through him. A yearning to break out in a desperate run and fly over the moonlit fields until he reached the foothills. And there would be Jenny waiting and beckoning him to run faster, until he finally reached her.

Jenny.

Jonathan.

Let's climb the mountain together.

Yes, Jenny. Yes.

Away from everybody.

Away, Jenny.

He bent over to kiss her . . . and then he heard the voice cut through. Low and harsh.

"Let me give you a tip," Mitch said.

"Go ahead."

"You behave, you'll get back on that plane alive."

"What do you mean by behave?" Jonathan asked.

"Just listen to what Carl has to say in the morning."

"I'll listen."

Mitch pushed the gun barrel hard in Jonathan's back. "Good. Because I like you. There's something about you that I like, Jonny Boy."

"What is it, Mitch?"

"Just keep moving along."

"I am."

They walked, their feet soft in the grass, and then he heard Mitch slowly speak again. "I guess you remind me of my kid brother."

Jonathan was silent.

"He was big and good-looking like you." Mitch continued. "Big and strong. And he liked books."

"Was?"

Mitch didn't speak.

"What happened?" Jonathan asked.

"He died."

"How?"

"Cancer."

"Oh." It must have hit you hard, Jonathan thought. Turned your life around. Completely around. Away from the light into the darkness.

"Your only brother?" Jonathan asked.

"That's right. There ain't no more. Gone. *Fini*."

And then he added bitterly, "A Jew doctor killed him."

Did he, Mitch? Jonathan wondered. Or did you have to find someone to hate for your brother's death? Was that it?

They stopped at the barn door, and Mitch opened it

and pointed with his gun. "Get in and don't turn on any lights."

"Okay," Jonathan said.

"Just lie down on the floor and get some sleep," Mitch said.

"I'll try to."

"That's it. Don't try to find a way out. There is no way out. Just stay put. Because Carl will know in the morning if you didn't. You going to be stupid and not listen to me, Jonny Boy?"

"I'll listen."

"That's it."

He pushed Jonathan inside the barn and shut the door. Jonathan was alone in the darkness.

Chapter
20

He lay there on the floor thinking of Mitch and of Carl and their smoldering hatred of all people who were not like them. A hatred that burned away everything that was human and decent within them.

And made them into Skinheads.

Skinheads.

"Skinheads," he said almost in a whisper.

And the word, said aloud, chilled him.

They end up killing or being killed.

And how will I end up? How?

Listen to Carl. What does he want to say to me? What does he want?

Jonathan lay there, his eyes open, trying to pierce the darkness. Finally his thoughts began to wander away from the dreaded Skinheads. He thought longingly of the beach and the sunny days at Southhampton. Of his grandfather.

And then he remembered.

One summer morning he had come down very late for breakfast, and he paused on the threshold of the huge, sunny room and then stood there listening to his mother and his grandfather talking.

They were sitting across the table from each other, and the servant who had just waited on them had left the room.

His grandfather was speaking in a low and firm voice. "He should be here for breakfast. I want him here."

"Jonathan was out very late last night, Father."

"No excuse."

"He's not a child anymore."

"He's my grandson."

"And you're trying to make him into your image. It just won't do."

Peter Atwood looked sharply at his daughter and then lifted his coffee cup and drank. Then he set his cup down firmly. His lips were moist and thin. "It will do," he said.

He picked up his napkin and delicately began to wipe his moist lips.

His daughter shook her head. "It won't," she protested. "He has some of his father's traits and he just—"

Atwood dropped the napkin and fiercely cut in. "I don't want to hear about his father. I told you Jonathan is my grandson. An Atwood. He'll take over when I'm gone. Everything."

"I know. But—"

He raised his hand commandingly. "No more. Be silent."

"All right, Father," she murmured.

Atwood looked across the table at his daughter. "And while we're on the subject. I've told you before. And I'll tell you again. You drink too much. Much too much. It's become obscene. Stop it. Or I'll have you put into a clinic."

Jonathan saw his mother's face become ashen.

"Do you hear me?" he demanded.

"I hear you, Father," his mother said in a low and harsh voice. "But let me remind you that it was you who caused me to—"

"Enough," Atwood shouted. His hand came down hard on the table, rattling the dishes.

She shivered as if he had struck her.

The servant had come to the doorway, eyes opened wide, and then he swiftly disappeared.

It was then that Jonathan decided to walk into the room.

"Sit down, Jonathan," his grandfather said coldly.

He sat and looked over to his mother and he saw tears in her eyes.

Soon she got up, and on the way out of the room, paused and kissed him on the forehead.

He watched her go, feeling bitter at his grandfather.

"Be on time in the future, Jonathan."

"Yes."

"And don't stand on thresholds overhearing conversations that you shouldn't be hearing."

Jonathan felt his back begin to stiffen. "I think you were very hard with her," he said.

Atwood lifted his eyes silently from his plate.

Jonathan spoke again. "What's wrong with the two of you?"

"Nothing."

"I wish you'd tell me, Grandfather."

"Jonathan."

"I want to know."

"It's none of your business."

"I believe it is."

His grandfather's Atwood blue eyes became icy. "Let it alone. I warn you. Don't try me, boy."

Jonathan shook his head grimly, his face white. "You must tell me. I'm not a boy anymore. I've a right to know."

"A right? You speak to me of rights in my house?"

"Yes, Grandfather. I do."

"Eat and be silent."

Jonathan was about to speak again when Atwood roared at him. "Silence!"

Jonathan slowly rose. "I don't want any breakfast. I've lost my appetite."

He saw the pain and the fury in the old man's eyes, but he turned away and went out of the room, hearing the old man cry, "Jonathan."

He left the huge house and walked the beach the rest of the morning, gazing out at the restless sea. When he returned, Atwood had gone to New York. The next day they were warm and close to each other again.

But he never found out. Not from his mother. And not from his grandfather.

And now, as he lay there in the dark barn remembering, he wondered what his mother meant when she said to her father that he had caused her to . . .

To do what, Mother? What? Your drinking? And what was it that made you drink so much and for so long a time? What, Mother? Did it have anything to do with me? My father? That quiet, bland man whom I rarely see and when I do, he has so few words to say to me. Or to anyone else.

I never could make him out, Mother. Nor you. What went wrong? What happened?

He lay there a long time thinking, thinking. Then he heard the distant wavering sound of a locomotive whistle, long and haunting. He listened to it until it was lost in the night.

His eyes closed and he slept. A restless sleep. He dreamed.

He was standing in the huge breakfast room and his grandfather and his mother were facing each other angrily. The two began to shout at each other, but he couldn't make out the words. They were too jumbled. Suddenly, the two became aware of Jonathan standing close to them. They turned. They looked silently down at him. And it was then that he realized that they were looking down at a very small and fearful child.

"Little Jonathan," Peter Atwood said softly.

"Little Jonathan," his mother murmured tenderly.

"My only grandchild."

"My only child."

Atwood put out his arms to his daughter, and she came tearfully into them.

"I'm sorry," he said. "Sorry I did it. Forgive me. I was wrong. So wrong."

"You did it for little Jonathan. For him."

He nodded sadly. "Yes. For little Jonathan."

And the two turned and gazed mournfully at Jonathan.

And he saw that he was the child. So very small. So very helpless.

His mother gently turned away from him and went over to a table and picked up a bottle of whiskey and then a glass. She poured the whiskey into the glass until it was full. Then she filled another glass with the amber liquid. It sparkled. She brought the second glass over to her father and gave it to him. Then she lifted her shimmering glass high. "To Jonathan," she said.

"To Jonathan," the old man echoed.

"We did it for him."

"For him."

"For him."

And with the words echoing in his mind, Jonathan awoke from his dream, the darkness still about him, chill and threatening.

He could sleep no more.

Chapter
21

The door of the barn partly opened and two figures entered silently, one after the other. A gun barrel glinted in the half-darkness. Jonathan shivered and tensed up. He could see the hard eyes of Carl. A panic came over him. He'll kill me now, he thought. They've decided to do it. To get rid of me. And I'm trapped. Trapped. No way out.

He waited for the sudden flash and the shattering sound, the bullet slamming into his head. But it didn't come. Just heavy silence.

He could hear their breathing.

Then one of the figures moved slowly to the partly opened door. He saw the whiteness of a hand as it reached out. Before the door closed, he could see that it was morning and the sky was gray and there were little patches of fog over the grassy fields. His eyes rested longingly on the fields. Then the door shut and it was absolute darkness again. But only for an instant. The lights went on, and Jonathan put his hand to his eyes and then let it fall to his side.

He was standing in a very large room with walls painted light blue.

Wooden folding chairs arranged in rows, facing a raised platform and on the platform an oblong table. A large American flag stood on one side of the table. On the wall behind it a large white banner. *America for Americans.*

While he gazed about him, the two stood by him, one on each side.

Mitch pointed to the banner. "Let's hear you read it," he said. He wore the red bandana on his bald, shining head.

"Go ahead," Carl said.

Jonathan stood there in silence.

Carl suddenly hit him hard on the wrist with the butt of the gun.

Jonathan drew back and winced in pain. Then his lips shut tight.

"Read it," Carl said grimly.

"Loud and clear," Mitch said.

"Let's hear it."

And Carl raised the gun butt again.

Jonathan looked at the banner. "American for Americans," he read aloud. His voice sounded strange and flat to him in the empty room.

"Give it more punch," Carl said.

"Do it, Jonny Boy."

"America for Americans," Jonathan said.

"Shout it. So the whole country can hear you. Shout

it,'' Carl said in his low and hard voice. "Let the Kikes, the Spics, and the Jigs hear it.''

Jonathan's jaw muscles moved, and then he closed his eyes and shouted the words.

The two clapped loudly.

"That's the way to do it, Jonny Boy," Mitch said.

"You're learning. The American Way," Carl said.

Looking at their cruel, intense faces, Jonathan felt bleak despair come over him. Who knows what they'll end up doing to me? he thought. I can't follow their twisted minds. I just can't.

Carl is the more dangerous of the two. I've got to watch him at all times. Then he felt Mitch pat him on the shoulder.

"I like you, Jonny Boy. You learn fast. Doesn't he, Carl?''

Carl didn't speak.

Mitch pointed proudly around him at the room. "What do you think about it all?'' he asked.

Jonathan didn't answer him.

"This is our headquarters. We're having a big, important meeting this Sunday. Strategy and tactics. Just like the military do.''

"Cut it out, Mitch," Carl said.

But Mitch went on. "They're coming from all over the Northwest. Carl is our commander. What do you think of that, Jonny Boy?''

"Impressive," Jonathan said.

Mitch grinned. "That's a good word. 'Impressive.' I like that.'' He turned to Carl. "A good word. We should use that in our literature. An impressive turnout.''

"I told you to stop talking," Carl said.

"What's wrong?"

Carl pushed him toward the door. "You talk too much. You've got a running mouth."

"Don't shove me, Carl."

"Then keep your mouth shut in front of him. I'll do the talking."

"Just don't shove."

The two stood facing each other.

But all the time Carl kept his eyes on Jonathan.

"Go to the house and make some breakfast," he said to Mitch.

"Just take it easy."

"Go ahead," Carl ordered.

"Okay," Mitch muttered, the anger still smoldering in his eyes.

"Close the door behind you."

Carl waited until Mitch closed the door behind him and then he pointed with his gun to the platform. "Get up there and sit at the table."

Jonathan stared at him. "What?"

Carl raised the gun menacingly. "Do it."

He watched Jonathan go up the three steps onto the platform and then walk over to the table and slowly sit down.

"That's it."

Carl moved over to the front row and sat down on one of the chairs.

He looked up at Jonathan, the gun resting in the palm of his hand. "Now I'm going to ask you some questions and you answer them. Listen and then answer."

Jonathan waited.

"You're being court-martialed."

"What?"

"You're an American, aren't you?"

"Yes."

"I'm going to find out how good an American you are. Whether you are a traitor to your country or not."

"Traitor?" Jonathan said.

"That's right."

Jonathan stared at the man in the camouflage jacket and pants and at the hard face and bald head. At the cold, cold eyes, a thin gleam at the center. You're mad, he thought. A mad dog running loose.

Then he heard Carl's voice. "Just answer the questions. And begin to pray that you give me the right answers. You got it, Rich Boy?"

Jonathan silently nodded.

"Rich Boy."

Carl looked up at him and a sudden fury came over the man.

"Rich Boy," he said again. "Rich Boy. You had it easy all your life. Supereasy. And I had nothing. Nothing. My father died in a coal mine. Ribs crushed in. Didn't leave us a dime. Not a thin dime."

His voice rose to a shout.

"We had nothing. Nothing. My mother died young. Worked out. And look at you. Look, Rich Boy. Your father and grandfather up to their eyes in dollar bills. Is that American. Is it? Answer me."

"It isn't," Jonathan said.

"It isn't," Carl said. He put his thick hand to his sweaty face and then drew it away, then slowly sat back in his chair.

When he spoke again, his voice was low and controlled and hard. "Why were you going to the detective's house?"

Jonathan didn't answer.

"Listen, Soldier. I can end the court-martial right now. Verdict death."

Jonathan paled.

"Then I'll put a bullet in your head, and nobody will ever know it. We'll bury your traitor body where nobody will ever find it. Is that clear to you?"

"Yes." Jonathan said. "It's clear."

"Answer the question."

"To get his help."

"Go on."

"To find out who murdered Alfred Kaplan."

Carl nodded grimly. "I see. And you were going to tell him that the Skinheads did it. Isn't that so?"

Jonathan didn't speak.

"Answer."

"Yes."

"The Skinheads did it. That's what the kook told you. Answer me."

"Yes."

Carl's voice became harsh. "Nobody believes her. Not even the detective. I know he doesn't. I know it. She's been to him before. She drew a blank with him."

There was a silence.

Then Jonathan spoke. "Why do you call her a kook?" he asked.

"Because she is one." Carl leaned forward to him. "You meet the girl in the airport. The first time. And you believe her. You ever see her before?"

"Never."

92

"Ever talk to her before? On the phone? Anywhere?"

"No," Jonathan said.

"And yet you believe her. What do you know about her?"

"Nothing."

"Nothing." Carl smiled, a grim, sardonic smile.

It's true, Jonathan thought. He's right. I know nothing about her. Only what she's told me. Only that.

He saw Carl raise his left hand with the tiny swastika on its thick wrist. And Jonathan remembered how Carl had raised that hand when he ordered Jenny to drive away and not come back. The man now waved his hand at Jonathan for emphasis.

"We have good reason for calling her a kook. Do you want to know what it is?" Carl asked.

"Yes."

"Because she had a breakdown. Did you know that?"

Jonathan looked at him.

"Did you? Answer me," Carl said.

"No," Jonathan said in a low voice.

"She didn't tell you?"

"No."

"Do you remember the scarf she wears around her neck?"

Jonathan didn't answer. Within him a chill had begun to spread.

"The pink scarf. She likes the color," Carl said.

"Yes."

"Do you know why she wears it?"

"She has a scar," Jonathan said.

"She has a scar," Carl echoed. Then he leaned forward in his seat, the overhead light shining on his skinhead. "She ever tell you how she got it?"

"No."

"She tried to kill herself. That's how."

"I don't believe you," Jonathan said. The words came out before he could stop them.

Carl's eyes flashed. "You don't?"

"That's what I said."

Carl's lips thinned and he slowly rose and faced Jonathan. His body was stiff and erect. His voice sharp and commanding. "You believe me, Soldier. Me. You have no other choice."

And if I don't?

"I'll read your thoughts for you," Carl said. "You believe her, you don't walk out of this room alive."

Jonathan was silent.

"Now I'm going to try to convince you to believe me and not the kook. And I'll know if I've done it or not. Don't try to fake it. It won't work with me."

Carl sat down again. He looked long at Jonathan, studying him. There was a chilling stillness in the room. The barrel of the gun gleamed in the cold light. When he spoke, it was in a voice that was low and almost soft. "Listen to me. And forget you ever met the kook. Can you do that?"

"I'll try," Jonathan said.

Carl nodded. "Do that, Soldier. Do that."

He paused and then spoke again. "We're not what she told you we are. We don't kill just to kill. No. Not at all. We're in a patriotic war to save our country. Your country and mine. We want a pure and white America. Is that clear to you?"

94

"It's clear," Jonathan said.

"What kind of America do you want? You see the Jews, the Jigs, the Puerto Ricans, the Spics, the Polacks, the Dagos, swarming over this beautiful land of ours like cockroaches. Is that the kind of America you want?"

I always thought America was for everyone, Jonathan thought. Regardless of race, creed, color, or origin. That we all share in this country of ours. That we all have the same rights.

He heard Carl speak again. "Hitler was right. He tried to tell us that you have to be pure to survive. Do you hear me? Pure inside and out."

How do you define pure? Jonathan wondered. How? And who is impure? Anyone who is not like you?

"Hitler was right. There are people who are born to lead. And people who are born to be led. Just look at a person's skin or nose, and it will tell you. There are people who should have the money and people who shouldn't. Your grandfather has a right to his money. Because he earned it with his brains and macho. And you have a right to it because you're in his bloodline. Your grandfather goes back to the *Mayflower*. Doesn't he?"

I don't know what that has to do with the right to lead and to be led, Jonathan thought. Or to have money and not have money.

"Do you follow me?" Carl said.

"Yes," Jonathan said. But to himself he said, No, I don't. Your logic is mad and inhuman. And completely un-American.

"Do you love your country?" Carl asked.

95

"Yes."

"With your heart and soul as we do. No. You don't."
He shook his bald head violently. "Because we're out
to purify it. You purify gold, don't you? You get rid of
the dregs."

And you are the gold. The pure, white, glistening
gold.

"We're soldiers in a patriotic war. We have more and
more of us enlisting. We have money coming to us.
And when the day is right, and that day will come, it
will, then we'll rise up and purify our country. With
arms, if necessary. Is that clear to you?"

"It's clear," Jonathan said.

So deadly clear.

"Soldiers only kill when they have to. You understand that?"

"Yes."

"I could have blown you away. But I'm doing my
best not to. You understand that, too?"

"Yes," Jonathan murmured.

"We did not kill Kaplan. Open your mind to that. I
can't stand dealing with closed minds. They drive me
up a wall. Open up. Do you hear me, Soldier?"

"I'm listening."

"Don't fake it," Carl said.

"I'm not. I'm listening."

"With an open mind?"

"Yes," Jonathan said.

"He was walking in a park at night and he was
mugged. By some Jigs. What's so unusual about that?
People get mugged in city parks. Especially at night.
Don't they?" Carl said.

"I guess they do."

"Don't guess. They get mugged. Period."

"They get mugged," Jonathan said.

Carl nodded approvingly, but his hard eyes held Jonathan. His voice was low and soft as he continued. "That's more like it. You're opening your mind. Keep doing it. I know what she told you. That Kaplan was writing a book about us. Isn't that so?"

"Yes," Jonathan said.

"She's told other people the same lie. Did you know that?"

"No."

"She showed you the title page. Right?"

"Yes."

Carl shook his head. "Garbage. Just plain garbage. She typed that page herself."

Jonathan stared at him.

"I can see that you're starting to believe, aren't you?" Carl said.

"Maybe."

Carl waved his hand at him. "Book? There is no book. Never was one."

Jonathan didn't speak.

"It's all in her sick mind."

"Yes," Jonathan murmured.

Carl's eyes lit up. "That's it, Soldier. Sick. Sick." He laughed harshly.

Jonathan looked away from him to the pale blue walls, a bleak feeling rising inside him, and then he slowly turned back to the Skinhead. The rows of empty wooden chairs were behind Carl. Jonathan imagined them filled with people, people with intense faces and cold eyes, eyes of black hatred, bald, shining heads.

He imagined Carl standing erect on the platform speaking to them. Shouting. "America for Americans." He heard the fervent applause, and then the applause faded away. Silence. He shivered.

Then Jonathan heard the man's low voice. "She had you fooled, didn't she?" Carl said.

"Yes."

Carl studied him and then spoke again. "Listen to me. We never touched Alfred Kaplan. I swear to you on my mother's grave. We didn't like him because he was a Jew. Jews are not pure white Americans. You know that, don't you?"

"Everybody knows that," Jonathan said.

Carl nodded. "Kaplan didn't like us. But it never went anywhere."

"You left him alone," Jonathan said.

"Sure we did. A professor in a university. We have bigger people to take care of. Why bother with him?"

"You called me at the hotel," Jonathan said.

Carl grinned sardonically. "And I had you believe that we killed Kaplan."

"Yes."

"Only to scare you off. We knew the kook would get to you. That's why we wanted you to take a plane out of here."

"And now?" Jonathan asked.

"Why not get on that plane? You stay here, you'd get the detective to listen. You'd get your grandfather in. He's a very powerful man."

"He can be when he wants to," Jonathan said.

98

"And we don't want him to." Carl slowly stood up, the gun tight in his hand. "Well, Soldier? Are you taking the plane out or do we have to bury you in some ravine where you'll rot for years to come?"

"You know the answer," Jonathan said.

"You tell me."

"I'll go home alive."

"And stay home," Carl said. "Or this time we'll kill the kook. You don't want that, do you?"

"I'll stay home," Jonathan said.

Carl slowly nodded. "Okay, Soldier. I'll book the flight for you."

"Today?"

"Yes." He looked long at Jonathan. Then he turned away from him and walked to the barn door. He opened it, and Jonathan could see again the gray morning sky and the patches of fog hovering over the wide fields.

The Skinhead paused at the open door, his figure outlined dark against the sky. "Tell me," he said.

Jonathan waited.

"What is Alfred Kaplan to you?"

"To me?"

"That's right." Carl said.

"Nothing that I know of."

"You're sure?"

"Yes," Jonathan said.

"Why did he have you come out here?"

"I don't know."

"It's a mystery to you?" Carl said.

"Yes."

"Did the detective have any idea?"

Jonathan shook his head. "He didn't even know the dead man was Alfred Kaplan."

"I see."

There was a short silence.

Then Carl spoke again. "But he knows now."

Jonathan nodded.

"What did Kaplan want to tell you?" Carl asked.

"I've no idea."

"You're leveling with me, Soldier?"

"You can see that I am," Jonathan said.

"I guess I can."

Then the dark figure said something that Jonathan never forgot. "Life is full of mysteries. Mysteries that finally kill us before we can solve them. Isn't that so?"

Jonathan didn't answer.

Then the Skinhead reached over and pulled the light switch.

The door shut.

Jonathan was left again in the darkness.

He began to shiver, violently.

And he said to himself, He almost killed me.

He almost did.

Chapter
22

Jenny.

He sat in the darkness and he thought of Jenny Mason and of what the Skinhead had said of her, with his cruel eyes and harsh laugh.

Kook. A sick mind. Sick. Sick.

Tried to commit suicide. The scar. The pink scarf that covers it from sight. Like a secret shame.

Jonathan's hands clenched and unclenched.

No. No. Why should I believe him? He lied to me. All lies. Lies.

They murdered Alfred Kaplan. Savagely beat him to death. They're savages. No matter what he says. I swear on my mother's gave that I . . . He can swear on a thousand mothers' graves, and I won't believe him.

I believe Jenny. Jenny.

You do? What do you know about her, Soldier? Tell me. What?

"Carl is right," Jonathan whispered. You see her once and you believe her. Once and you put your life on the line for her. Only once, you fool.

They're not the lunatics. You are. You're the mad one.

He's right. The Skinhead is right. What do I know about her? What? I always come back to this question. Always to this.

Jonathan rose from the chair and stared into the impenetrable darkness, his face agonized.

"Jenny," he whispered. Then he said her name again. This time his voice was a cry. "Jenny."

The word echoed against the walls of the empty room, then slowly, slowly faded away.

He stood there for a few moments longer, and then despairingly sat down again.

Stillness was all around him. And the question would not leave him, would not give him peace.

What do I know about her?

Only one thing.

Only one.

That from the instant I saw her I couldn't stop thinking about her.

Only that.

Jenny.

Chapter
23

The door opened and Mitch came in, whistling a low, poignant tune. As he turned on the lights, he stopped whistling and called out to Jonathan.

"How's it going, Jonny Boy?"

Jonathan looked over at the stocky figure with the thick face and the red bandana around the bald head, the stubble of brown beard on the square chin. And the smile on the thick lips. A pleasant smile. But behind it all, a haunting sadness deep in the eyes.

Jonathan thought of the dead brother. Mitch's brother who had died young, of cancer. So very young. You must have loved him a lot, Mitch, to have turned you so bitter against the rest of the world.

But where did you get the other dose of deadly poison? Who put that into you? Fellows like Carl? They're the ones who really twist the minds and darken the hearts of good, decent people. They're the ones.

You're just a follower. You were wounded and bleeding and Carl stumbled into your life. Just at the right time. Isn't that how it worked out?

"So-so, Mitch," Jonathan said.

"I've brought you some breakfast. Hungry?" Mitch asked.

"Yes."

But in being a follower, you become just as cruel and savage as Carl. And you get blood all over you. That's the price you pay. A very bitter price.

Inside of you, Mitch, you've begun to die. Carl is already dead. Don't you realize that? Think, Mitch. Think. You can still turn it around. You can.

The man came over to the platform, carrying a tray of dishes, balancing it in the grip of his thick, strong hand. In his other hand, Jonathan could see the gun. Mitch came up the steps and set the tray on the table.

"Eat and be happy," he said.

"I'll try, Mitch."

"Do it."

Mitch went down the stairs and over to one of the chairs and sat down. He took out a cigarette and lit it.

"Carl tells me you listened to him," he said.

Jonathan ate silently.

"We'll put you on a plane at five o'clock. How's that?"

"Okay," Jonathan said.

"And stay on it this time."

"I will, Mitch."

"Stay away from Seattle. The climate's no good for you."

"I know that now."

"How're the eggs?"

"Couldn't be better. You're a good cook."

Mitch blew out some smoke and grinned. "That's what I am. I worked as a short-order cook all over the Northwest. A lot of one-arm joints."

"Still do it?"

Mitch shook his head. "Don't have to. We have some money people behind us."

Jonathan looked at him. "You do?"

Mitch nodded. "Sure thing. They believe as we do. All the way down the line."

"Oh."

"Maybe if you talk to your grandfather, you'll get him to give us some money. We're doing good things for this country."

"I know," Jonathan said quietly.

"The country needs purification. Always remember that word."

"Yes. *Purification*."

"You'll speak to him?" Mitch asked.

"My grandfather?"

"That's right. Peter Atwood."

"I'll do it," Jonathan said.

Mitch nodded. "I have a feeling he thinks like we do."

Jonathan paused in his eating. "Why?"

"I don't know. It's just a gut feeling."

"Oh."

"And my gut feelings are pretty good," Mitch said.

"They are?"

"On the mark. Almost always."

You're wrong this time, Mitch. I'm sure you're wrong.

And then again, in certain areas of thought, you never know where Peter Atwood stands. You never really know. He drops a wall in front of you. And he never takes it down.

"Eat up, Jonny Boy."

"Okay, Mitch."

Mitch sat back in his chair, smoking and watching Jonathan. A gentle look came into his eyes.

"You eat like my brother did," he said. "Slow and easy. Taking your good time."

Jonathan didn't speak.

"You had me on edge last night, Jonny Boy," Mitch said quietly.

"How, Mitch?"

"I was afraid I'd be hearing a gunshot."

"In my head?"

"Dead center."

He smoked.

There was a silence.

He suddenly spoke again. "Don't be a hero. There are no more heroes in this screwed-up world of ours. You try to be one and you're blown away. You understand, Jonny Boy?"

"Yes, Mitch."

"Just go home and sit on a sunny beach and use up your grandfather's money. Should take you a lifetime."

"I'll do that," Jonathan said.

"Just use up his money and be happy."

"Right."

"Let the world sail by and forget it. Let it sink in the ocean. You keep sitting on the beach," Mitch said.

"In the sun."

"In the sun. How's the coffee?"

"Couldn't be better."

Mitch smiled. "I put egg shells into it and then strain them out. Gives it a special flavor."

"It does."

"A trick my mother taught me. I come off a Minnesota farm. Snow country."

"Is the farm still there?" Jonathan asked.

Mitch shook his head. "Gone. All gone. Just me and my brother. And then he went. I buried him. Then I got into a car and drove away. Left the house, the land, all standing there. I never went back. And I never will."

"Maybe you should."

Mitch's big hand opened and closed. "Gone, Jonny Boy. Gone. *Fini. Kaput. Sayonara.* I'm too far down the road. There is no going back."

He was silent again.

Jonathan put down his cup. "It was good. Very good."

Mitch didn't say anything.

"Where is Carl now?"

He turned back to Jonathan. "Carl?"

"Yes."

"Went into Seattle. On something important. He's always doing something important. Like a little king." A smoldering look had come into his eyes. "King." He crushed out his cigarette and flung it away.

"You don't like him too much, do you, Mitch?" Jonathan said.

The man nodded grimly. "He can be hard to take at times."

"I can see that."

Mitch shrugged his shoulders. "But I guess that's how leaders are. Hitler was the same way. But he sure knew how to lead."

Mitch lit another cigarette and broke the wooden matchstick in his fist. "A bit off the wall at times. And that's how Carl is. He can go off the wall, and then you'd better watch out."

He sat there looking straight ahead of him, his face grim and thoughtful.

"He wanted to be a lawyer," he suddenly said in a low voice.

"Who, Mitch?"

A wistful look had come into the man's eyes. "Wasn't interested in making big money. Not like the other kids who go into law these days. Not like those yuppies in their expensive suits and their attaché cases. Their bars and their expensive apartments." He shook his head. "Just wanted to be good enough to help the poor and the defenseless. That's all he wanted to do."

Jonathan realized that the man was talking about the dead brother. "The poor and the defenseless are generally the minorities, Mitch," he said.

"I know. He used to say *pro bono* a lot. You know what that means?"

"Yes, Mitch," Jonathan said gently. "It's Latin. *Pro bono populi.*"

"That's it."

"For the good, the benefit of the people," Jonathan said.

"I get it."

"He would have been a public defender," Jonathan said. "A lawyer the court appoints when the accused has no money to get himself one. In some states it's called *legal aid*."

Mitch nodded. "He would have been a good one. I tell you, one of the best."

"I'm sure, Mitch."

"I was putting money aside for him. For his education. And then when he died, I went to Vegas and blew it all on the crap tables." Mitch paused and then went on. "Every single cent of it. I would hit a winning streak, but I wouldn't stop and leave the table. I wanted to lose it all. All of it."

"I know what you mean," Jonathan said.

"It was like the money was cursed. And I wanted to get rid of it." Mitch shook his head sadly. "He was too good and too gentle for this brutal, savage world. That's why he went down. He was doomed from the start." His face tightened and he turned away and stopped speaking.

There was a deep silence.

In the distance, Jonathan could hear the muffled sound of an airplane. He listened to it until the sound was gone. All the while he kept gazing at the man sitting in the chair below him, the red bandana around the bald head, the gun in his lap.

Mitch, he thought sadly. Mitch, listen to me. Your brother wanted to defend the very same people you now hate and want to clear out of the country. Purification. You're talking of the Blacks, the Hispanics, the Jews, the Chinese, the Koreans, the . . . It's almost endless.

Your brother would have been horrified to see you now. To hear the way you talk. The way you act. You Skinheads beat Alfred Kaplan to death.

You would have broken your brother's heart. Just as yours is broken now. Mitch. Listen to me.

But Jonathan sat there and said nothing.

Then he heard Mitch sigh and saw him slowly get up.

"You feel better now?" Mitch asked. "Your gut in good shape?"

Jonathan nodded. "Thanks, Mitch. It was a good breakfast."

"And that's coming from a dude who's eaten in some real fancy places."

"I have."

"And how does this one rack up?"

"Tops," Jonathan said.

"Four stars?"

"I'll give it five."

Mitch grinned. "Leave the tip on the tray."

"You take MasterCard?" Jonathan asked.

"No. Only hard cash."

Mitch reached up and took hold of the tray. "What kind of tip do you generally leave?"

"Twenty percent, Mitch."

"That's pretty steep. I was lucky to get ten. Did you know that Jews and Blacks are good tippers?"

"No."

"You wouldn't. You never worked a day in your life."

"That's true, Mitch."

Mitch looked at him, a smile in the haunted eyes. "How does it feel to live that way?" he asked.

"Feels good."

"Yes," Mitch said in a low voice. "I guess it does."

He turned toward the door. "Think of your grandfather and purification."

"I will," Jonathan said.

"Money, Jonny Boy. We can use it."

"I'll try my best with him."

"Good enough," Mitch said.

He walked to the door and was about to open it, but he stopped and turned. He looked back at Jonathan. A shadow had come over his face and figure.

Jonathan could barely hear his voice when he spoke. The words seemed to hover in the air.

"I've done some real bad things in my life. And seen some bad ones. And I can handle that," Mitch said. "But there's one thing I don't want to see happen."

Jonathan waited.

The man spoke again. "I don't want to see you dead. You're not out of the woods yet." His voice rose just a bit. Now Jonathan heard every word clearly. "Not when there's a Carl around. He's off the wall. So you take it easy with him. Very easy."

I know that, Jonathan said to himself. I know, Mitch.

"Be careful how you talk to him," Mitch said. "Don't trust him even when he smiles at you. Be careful."

Yes, Mitch.

A sad, haunted look came over the man's face.

"Anything can set him off. And there's nothing I can do to stop it. You understand, Jonny Boy?"

"Yes, Mitch," Jonathan murmured.

"It would be like seeing my brother die again. I can't handle that. You remind me of him too much."

He stopped speaking and stood there looking at Mitch, his shadow long on the bare floor.

"He's off the wall."

The man opened the door and went out.

Chapter
24

The figure stood outlined against the dull gray light of the afternoon sky, and Jonathan immediately sensed that something had gone wrong.

Then the lights went on and he saw that it was Carl standing there, looking directly at him. A searching look in the cold blue eyes.

"How's it going, Soldier?" The voice was soft and pleasant, but there was something in it that sent a chill through Jonathan. A chill of fear.

"Okay."

"Only okay?"

Jonathan didn't answer.

The man's bald head gleamed under the light. He stood erect in his camouflage jacket and pants. His black boots shone.

"Mitch feed you?" Carl asked.

"Yes."

In his right hand Carl held his gun tight. His left hand was closed into a fist.

"A good meal?" he asked.

"Yes," Jonathan said.

"You hungry now?"

"A bit."

"Well, you'll eat at the airport."

"All right."

Carl stood looking at him. A strange gleam came into his eyes. "You can approach me, Soldier," he said.

Jonathan went slowly over to him.

"Stop where you are. You're close enough."

Jonathan stood still.

Carl opened his big fist, and Jonathan saw in the palm of the thick hand a crumpled pink scarf.

"Jenny," he whispered.

The man smiled. "Your girl friend. She sent it to you."

"What did you do to her?" Jonathan said.

Carl shook his skinhead. "Nothing. I told you she sent it. To remember her by." He held out his hand with the scarf in it. "She won't be at the airport to see you off."

"You killed her," Jonathan said fiercely.

"No."

"You did."

"You're getting too close. Step back, Soldier."

He pointed the gun at Jonathan's chest.

Jonathan moved back, his hands clenched.

"Just stay where you are," Carl said.

"You killed her. Why? What did she do to you?"

"Control yourself, Soldier."

"Why?" Jonathan shouted.

"I told her to stay away from the airport. So she sent you this. That's all there is to it."

"I don't believe you," Jonathan said.

"You don't?"

"No."

"You have no choice. Take the scarf."

Jonathan didn't move. His face was pale and tight.

Carl raised the gun again. "It's an order, Soldier."

Jonathan reached his hand out and took the scarf.

"That's better. When you get home you can write her and thank her for it."

Jonathan was silent.

Carl smiled. "You must learn to believe me," he said.

"Yes," Jonathan murmured bitterly.

Carl motioned to the open door. "All right. We're ready to get out of here. Start moving, Soldier."

Jonathan walked slowly past him, through the open door and out under the dull gray sky. A desolate feeling within him. The scarf felt warm in his hand.

As he looked past the wide, level fields to the towering mountain, he thought of Jenny.

Jenny. What did he do to you? What? Are you still alive? You have to be.

"Jenny," he whispered.

Then he tenderly folded the scarf and put it gently into his pocket.

I'll see you again. I will. It can't end up any other way. It just can't, Jenny.

He heard Carl's harsh voice. "Keep moving. We haven't much time left."

115

Jonathan walked silently along the grassy path to the farmhouse. Carl was close behind him.

As he walked, he wondered with dread, am I being taken to the airport? Or has this mad dog changed his mind? Has he? He's off the wall, Mitch said. And he is. He is.

Something has happened. I can feel it. Maybe I should make a run for it? Turn and hit him and run. Catch him by surprise.

But then I'll get a bullet right in my back. I'm trapped. Trapped. And there's nothing I can do about it. Nothing.

I always believed that you can do something about your destiny. It's in your hands. That's what my grandfather always taught me. It's up to you, Jonathan. Your fate is always up to you. You're an Atwood and the Atwoods always made their own destiny. You can, too. You will.

Jonathan heard the low swishing of grass as Carl walked softly behind him. His face darkened. Lies. All lies, Grandfather. We're no better than insects. Ants. Flies. Cockroaches. In the end we're squashed flat just as they are. There is no escape. We die in our own blood. It's all lies, Grandfather.

"Go to the car," Carl ordered.

Jonathan looked up and saw ahead of him the white car standing on the pebbled driveway, Mitch leaning against it, waiting for them to come up to him.

As Jonathan approached, he saw that the man's face was flat and impassive.

He didn't say a word to Jonathan.

"We're ready to take off, Carl."

116

"Okay."

Mitch opened the front door of the car and was about to step in when Carl spoke again. "I'll drive," he said.

Mitch turned slowly and looked at him. "Why?" he asked.

"You heard me. Sit in the back with him."

"What's going on, Carl?"

"Sit there."

"I don't get it," Mitch said.

"You don't have to. Just do as I say."

They stood facing each other.

"We're taking him to the airport, Carl."

"I know."

"The airport," Mitch said in a hard voice. He tugged at the red, sweaty headband. His bald head glinted in the dull afternoon light.

"Get in with him," Carl said coldly.

Mitch still stood there, looking at the man.

"It's an order," Carl said.

"Yeah."

"Well?"

Mitch glanced over to Jonathan. Then he seemed to sigh. "Okay, Carl," he murmured.

He turned and pushed Jonathan into the back seat and then got in beside him.

"You're not out of the woods, Jonny Boy," he said.

Jonathan stared at him in terror.

But there was no mercy in the man's eyes.

Chapter
25

They rode in complete silence, each one a prisoner of his own thoughts.

Then suddenly Carl began to sing in a soft, cruel voice.

> Blacks
> Blacks
> Blacks
> They call them Blacks now
> How nice
> How cute
> They call them Blacks now
> Blacks
> Blacks
> Blacks
> But where do they come from?
> Where?

He stopped singing and looked back at Jonathan.

"Where do they come from?"

Jonathan's face was pale and grim. He did not answer.

Carl laughed low. "The jungle. Sing it, Mitch."

"You were supposed to turn off there," the man said quietly.

"Sing it," Carl said.

"That was the highway to the airport. You just passed it," Mitch said.

"We're not going there now."

"What?"

"We're making a short stop."

"Carl."

"That's how it's going to be."

"Carl," he said again. And then he shut his lips tight and was silent.

Jonathan sat there with a growing dread as the car headed through a tree-lined, deserted road in the direction of the mountains. Mile after mile. The eerie, desolate silence was broken only by the sound of the tires on the dirt surface of the level road. An endless, terrifying sound. He looked out at the gray sky. It had turned bleak and cold. Jonathan bent his head and would not look anymore. The car sped on.

When he looked up again, Jonathan saw that they had come to the foothills. The car began to slow down. And Jonathan saw it enter a dark and silent forest. He felt a tremor go through him as they drove between the high trees with their thick, overhanging branches. The thick leaves like a pall over them.

He put his hand into his pocket, his fingers searching

and then finding the soft silk of the scarf. I'll never see you again, Jenny, he said to himself. Never.

For an instant he had a mad vision of a sunny beach and sparkling ocean water and Jenny lying on the white sand at his side.

Carl drove the car into a little clearing and then turned off the motor.

The vision was gone. Shattered. Like a mirror into a hundred silvery pieces. And now only bitter reality remained.

Carl got out of the car and came to the back door and opened it. "We're here. Get out, Soldier."

Jonathan sat there in icy terror and didn't move.

Carl's lips thinned. "Drag him out, Mitch," he ordered.

"Just what are you planning to do, Carl?" Mitch said.

"What do you think?"

Mitch shook his head grimly and stepped out of the car. "I don't go for this."

"You'd better," Carl said. There was a cold gleam in his pale blue eyes. He pushed Mitch aside and reached into the car and hit Jonathan hard across the jaw with the butt of his gun. Jonathan fell back and cried out.

"Don't sit there. Get out of the car," Carl said.

Jonathan slowly put his hand to his jaw and drew it away. There was a trickle of blood. But his face ached with a dull, searing pain. He looked despairingly at the Skinhead standing erect before him.

Then he heard Carl's harsh, commanding voice. "I give you an order, Soldier."

He saw the gun butt being raised again.

"Well?"

Jonathan felt a sickening feeling in his stomach as he slowly got out of the car and stood facing the Skinhead. A nausea of fear began to sweep over him. He felt that he was about to faint. He clenched his fists tight and held himself rigid.

"Start walking," Carl said, pointing to a nearby cluster of trees. The leaves shivered in a passing wind. Then they were still.

"Walk, I said."

Jonathan looked desperately at Mitch.

Their eyes met.

Save me, Mitch. Please.

But the man turned away from him.

Again he heard Carl's harsh voice. "Move, Soldier."

Jonathan started to walk slowly to the trees.

"Why, Carl?" Mitch suddenly said.

"Stay out of this."

"Why? Did she get to the detective? Is that it?"

"He knows we took Jonny Boy," Carl said.

"So he knows. Put him on the plane and let him go home."

Carl pushed Jonathan along. "We're getting rid of him. So they'll never find him."

"Carl."

"We're in for a bad rap if they do," Carl said.

"Just listen to me, Carl."

"No."

"I'm telling you let him go. He'll never come back."

Carl gripped Mitch's jacket in his big fist. His face white with anger. "I said to her if she went to the detective her boyfriend would be dead meat. Didn't I say that? Didn't I?''

"You did," Mitch said.

"Well?"

Mitch looked at him and was silent.

Carl let go of the jacket. "We'll do what we have to do and then get out of here," he said.

He turned sharply to Jonathan. "Stand against that tree. Your back to it."

Jonathan sucked in his breath and then leaned against the trunk of the tree. He held Jenny's scarf tight in his hand. He thought of her and closed his eyes.

Then he heard Carl's voice again. "Soldier, this is a military execution. You have a choice to be blindfolded or not. What is it?"

Jonathan didn't speak.

Carl turned to Mitch. "Tie the scarf around his eyes."

"You're going ahead with it," Mitch said.

"Yes. And then we're going up the mountain and getting rid of the body."

"In one of the gullies."

"Right."

"Where he'll never be found."

"Never," Carl said. "Tie the scarf and let's get it over with."

Mitch went over to Jonathan and took the scarf from his hand and as he did, Jonathan opened his eyes. For a shattering instant they stood there gazing at each other. And a sad, haunted expression came over the man's rugged face. He dropped the scarf and turned to Carl, his gun tight in his hand.

122

"No, Carl. I'm not going along with this."

"Mitch. Mitch, don't be a fool."

Mitch grimly shook his head. "I'm afraid there's nothing else I can do, Carl."

Then he shouted. "Run, Jonny Boy. Run."

Jonathan swung about and ran headlong into the woods.

And then he heard the shots.

They echoed against the sky.

Then the silence rushed in.

Chapter
26

His breath came in sharp, painful gasps. He felt that he could run no more. His throat was parched and dry.

It was then that he saw the gleam of water through the trees. He forced himself to run to the stream, and then he threw himself down on the water's edge and drank thirstily.

When he was done, he lay there panting, listening intently. No sound but that of the wind gently sighing through the silent trees.

I've got to rest, he said to himself. Just a few more seconds. And then go on again. Until I find a road or a highway. A house. A telephone.

If Mitch killed him, then I'll be all right. But if Carl . . . ?

He trembled and didn't complete the thought.

Jonathan got to his knees and listened again. Only the silence of the still forest. He rose to his feet and started running again. This time he followed the course of the stream.

Sooner or later it will lead me to a house or a road. It has to.

He stopped again to catch his breath and rest. He leaned against the trunk of a tree, and as he did he thought of Mitch, and of the haunted look deep in his eyes.

"Mitch," he whispered.

And he saw again the man standing before him, about to tie the scarf. The haunted, haunted look. The scarf fluttering to the ground like a wounded bird, fluttering and then lying still.

The haunted, haunted look.

Mitch, he said to the man. Mitch, you couldn't go through with it. Just couldn't. There was still something left within you. Something from the time when you were good and decent. When you worked a farm and had shining plans for the future. For your brother and you. Carl hadn't killed that in you. Not yet. Something was still left.

I wish I had met you then. When you were on the farm and—

Suddenly Jonathan leaned forward and listened. He thought he had heard a low rustle in the forest behind him. The soft crackle of little branches. Then the silence came in again.

Jonathan took a deep breath and began running again. His feet thudding along the wet bank. Thudding. Thudding.

The stream took a sudden turn, and Jonathan saw

ahead of him a lonely dirt road that led away from the water. The shadows of the late afternoon lay over it.

He hesitated an instant and then decided to leave the stream and the forest and follow the road. He ran along it, a lone figure under a gray, darkening sky. The trees flanking the road began to thin out, and it was then that he saw the sloping slate roof of a house. He ran until he came to it and then stopped, his heart beating fast.

It was a small green and white wooden house, newly painted, with a tiny well-kept garden in front. Two wooden rockers were on the porch. He stood there breathing heavily, and then he moved slowly up the front steps.

Jonathan knocked on the front door.

He waited. But no one answered.

All the time he kept looking desperately down the shadowy dirt road.

He turned and knocked again.

Finally, he put his hand to the doorknob and turned it. The door opened.

Jonathan called out, his voice sounding flat and hollow, "Anybody here?"

There was no answer.

He stepped further into the house. "Hello?"

Only silence.

He walked quickly through the living room and then into a back room. There he saw a desk and on it some strewn white papers and a small American flag on a tiny stand. Next to it was a car sticker with the words: *America for Americans.*

He trembled and was about to turn and run out of the house when he saw the telephone at the far end of the desk. A thin, dying ray of the sun fell upon it. The rest of the room was in shadow.

Jonathan sighed in relief and went over to the phone. When he picked up the black receiver it felt cold to his hand. He dialed zero and with held breath waited for the operator to come on. Time seemed to freeze. His hand began to shake.

"Police," he whispered.

Get me the police. It's a matter of life and death. Please speak to me. Please.

And it was then that he heard the low voice steal into the room, like a soft, chilling wind.

"Put it down."

Jonathan shivered and turned.

"Down, Soldier," Carl said.

Jonathan let the receiver fall onto its hook. And with that harsh sound he knew that he was about to die. No escape this time.

There was a savage gleam in the Skinhead's eyes. Blood was on the thick hand that gripped the gun. Dried blood. His face was a tight, gray mask. The lips thin and colorless. When he spoke, his voice was a ghostly whisper.

"Your luck's run out, Soldier. You came to the wrong house. It belongs to one of my Skinheads."

Jonathan kept staring at him with bleak despair.

"He's in Seattle now. Works for the University. That's how we found out about Alfred Kaplan's lying, vicious book. We're everywhere, you rich fool. Everywhere." Spit dribbled from his lips. "Everywhere. How did you think we found out so much about you? From the detective's son, Jed Ward. He's one of us. He knew every move his father was making. Every move. Fathers don't know their own children. Did your father know you? Answer me!''

Carl laughed but no sound came. Then the lips closed over the silent laughter. He stiffened and stood erect, a savage gleam in his pale blue eyes.

He slowly raised the gun. The barrel glinted as he pointed it at Jonathan's chest.

"I'm going to execute you now. This time Mitch won't save you.''

"Mitch,'' Jonathan murmured.

"Dead.''

And as Carl said the word, a sudden rage exploded within him. "You killed him, you rich fool!'' He shivered with fury. "You pulled the trigger.'' His voice rose. "You. You did it!''

He lunged forward and hit Jonathan hard on the forehead with the butt of the gun.

"A bullet is too good for you,'' he shouted. "Too good.''

He savagely struck Jonathan again, and Jonathan staggered and fell to his knees. His senses swirled. He looked up through a mist and saw the shimmering figure above him and the white hand raised with the gun butt in its grasp.

He heard the wavering words. "I'm going to beat you to death. Just as I did with the Jew Kaplan.''

Jonathan rolled to one side, and the blow struck him on the shoulder. He lunged and grabbed the man by the legs. With his last desperate strength he pulled hard, and the Skinhead fell backward to the floor. The gun dropped from the open hand with a clatter.

Jonathan pushed the man from him and slowly rose. He kicked the gun away. Then he waited with a cold fury for the Skinhead to get to his feet. Waited with the fists of his big hands clenched. The knuckles were white. Blood streamed from his forehead down onto his cheeks.

"Now we're even," he said as he faced the Skinhead. And he saw the look of fear come into the man's eyes. "We're even," Jonathan shouted.

He hit the Skinhead hard on the jaw and then again on the mouth. Two triphammer blows.

The man groaned in pain and swayed. He swung desperately at Jonathan but Jonathan ducked and then hit the Skinhead another jarring blow. The man gasped and slowly sank to one knee, his bald head bowed.

"Jenny Mason," Jonathan said.

The man looked dazedly up at him.

"What did you do to her?" Jonathan demanded.

"Nothing." The voice was a low, defeated murmur.

Jonathan stood grimly over him. "Tell me."

"The scarf. Just took the scarf," Carl said.

"To torture me with it? That it?"

"Something like that."

"Just a little fun with your cruelty?"

The man was silent.

Jonathan clenched his fist and raised it. "You're lying," he said.

The man fearfully flinched away from him. "She's in Seattle. At the University. I swear it to you."

"On your mother's grave?" Jonathan asked sardonically.

"You've got to believe me."

"Sure."

"She lives in a dormitory there. She's all right."

"Get up on your feet."

He watched as the Skinhead rose and then he roughly pushed him to the desk. "Sit on that chair."

Jonathan took a sheet of paper and then a pen.

"Here. I want you to write," he said.

The man looked fearfully up at him. "What?"

"Just these words." Jonathan put the pen in his hand. "Write. I killed Alfred Kaplan. And my fellow Skinhead, Mitch."

The man dropped the pen onto the desk. He shook his head. "No," he said.

Jonathan quietly gazed at him and then he went over to the gun, stooped, and picked it up. He came back to the desk.

"Pick up the pen," he said.

"No."

"Watch me," he said.

Then he removed the cartridges from the gun, one by one, leaving only the last one left in the cylinder. He put the barrel to the shaven head, his finger curled around the trigger.

"Okay. Sweat and pray each time I pull the trigger," Jonathan said.

The Skinhead trembled violently. A ghostly pallor was on his battered face. He couldn't speak.

"It could be the first pull. The second. The third . . . or the last. But a bullet is going to rip into your skull. Well?"

"You won't do it," the man whispered.

130

"Why not?" Jonathan said very quietly. But his eyes were cold and wild.

"Because you won't."

Jonathan smiled. A cruel, bitter smile.

"Because I'm not like you?" he said. "You make a mistake there, my friend. A deadly mistake."

He laughed. A harsh laugh. It echoed through the shadowy room.

"You've made me into an animal," Jonathan said. "Just like you. No difference. I've come down to your savage level. Believe me."

He pulled the trigger and the man screamed in terror.

There was an empty click.

"You're lucky this time," Jonathan smiled and he pointed grimly to the pen.

"Pick it up and write."

His finger tightened on the trigger.

"Don't. Don't," the Skinhead moaned. "I'll do it."

Jonathan watched him as he wrote the words.

"Now sign your name."

Then he picked up the phone and dialed for the police.

Chapter
27

He never said a word about his son. Just sat there talking about the Skinheads.

"That Carl is going to jail for a long, long time. And there'll be some others going with him."

Ward's face had a grayish pallor to it. His voice had a deadness.

"There's a lot of work ahead. I'd like to take early retirement and let others do it. But I'm going on. Until I sweep those lice out of this area. Each and every one of them."

He looked away from Jonathan and out of the window.

The morning was gray and dismal.

"That book that Kaplan wrote. I'm going to need help getting it published," Ward said. "It's needed. Needed so that people can read and see what's going on under their very noses. Sometimes you're so blind

that you can't see what's right there before you." His
voice almost broke. "You just don't see it."

And then he said again, "You don't see."

He looked straight at Jonathan and a steely, desperate
look came into his eyes. "What's with your generation?
What?"

Jonathan didn't answer.

"I gave him everything he wanted. Everything. What
went wrong? What?"

There was a heavy stillness. The man sighed deeply.
"You'd better go," he said.

Jonathan silently left the office, the image of the desolate detective haunting him.

Chapter

28

They were sitting under a large elm tree, looking out over the calm lake. The sun lay softly upon the clear water, making it shimmer.

His arm was around her shoulder.

Then he spoke.

"When I pulled the trigger, I knew the chamber was empty. I knew exactly where the last bullet was. And I also knew that he would give in before I got to it."

Then he sighed and said in a low voice, "But he did pull me down to his level. He sure did, Jenny."

She turned to him. "No, Jonathan. He couldn't."

"He did. He pushed me too hard. And then I thought of you, and that shoved me over the edge."

He looked gently at her.

She shook her head slowly. "Carl told you the truth. He didn't touch me. I was always terrified of him. He wanted the scarf, and I gave it to him. But he didn't touch me this time."

"This time?"

She didn't speak.

"What do you mean, Jenny?"

Her hand went to her scarf defensively.

"Jenny."

She had turned her face from him.

"Jenny," he said again.

And now he saw the anguish and the pain deep in her large eyes.

She spoke in a low, tortured voice. "It's in the past, Jonathan. A past I never want to think about again." Her hand fell away from the scarf. "It's gone, Jonathan. Gone forever."

He felt his heart go cold.

Is it, Jenny? Couldn't you tell me? Couldn't you? And he knew deep within him that she never would.

"All right, Jenny," he said softly.

"Some day I'll tell you."

He shook his head. "No, Jenny. Let it be."

"Thanks, Jonathan."

She kissed him gently and then drew back and gazed sadly at his bruised face.

"What is it?" he asked.

"You've been through so much," she said. "And it was all my fault."

"No."

"I should have let you go home."

"No, Jenny."

"I got you into all of this. I did." There were tears in her eyes. "You'll be going back soon?"

"This evening," he said.

"Oh."

And then they were silent again.

Far out on the lake a sailboat skimmed along. He watched it and thought of a white bird. A delicate white-feathered bird. Then he heard her voice.

"Jonathan."

"Yes?"

"There is something I have to tell you."

She paused and then drew in a deep breath.

He waited.

She spoke again. "Something I swore that I wouldn't."

She rose to her feet and stood gazing out at the water.

He slowly rose, too.

She spoke without turning to him. "It's about Alfred Kaplan."

"Yes?"

"He is dead. And I'm breaking my word to the dead. But I can't let you leave without your knowing the truth."

Within him a chill had started to spread. "The truth about what, Jenny?"

She turned and looked at him. Her face had turned pale. "You say you're coming back. But who knows if I'll ever see you again," she said. "Life is so full of bitter disappointments."

"The truth about what, Jenny?" he said again and his voice shook.

"He was your father."

Jonathan stared at her.

"He was," she repeated.

He still didn't speak.

"He wanted to see you before he died. He wanted to look into your eyes with his last fading strength. To look and then he would know if he could tell you the truth. Then he would know if you would or would not accept him as your father."

"Accept him?" Jonathan asked.

"He feared that you wouldn't. Feared it more than anything in his life."

Jonathan clenched and unclenched his hands.

"He had let you grow up as an Atwood. But he never stopped loving you. Never, Jonathan."

"Jenny," he whispered.

"And he never stopped loving your mother. She loved him. She was forced to give him up."

"Forced? What happened?"

"Your grandfather destroyed the marriage."

"No," he said.

"He used his influence to hound your father out of every university he tried to teach in. Until he gave up in despair and came out here."

Jonathan bowed his head and couldn't look at her.

"Your mother married again," Jenny said, "and you were never told the truth. Never. Because that's how Peter Atwood wanted it."

Jonathan turned away from her to the lake. The dazzling sunlight on the water blinded him. He put his hands to his eyes.

"Jonathan."

"Why?" he said. And the word came from his very soul.

She didn't answer him.

"Why did my grandfather do it?" Jonathan said.

She still didn't answer him.

"Jenny."

"Can't you guess?"

Now he knew but he didn't speak.

"Can't you, Jonathan?"

"Let me alone, Jenny," he said bitterly.

She put her hand out to him.

"Let me alone, Jenny," he said.

"Jonathan."

"Please," he said in a broken voice.

And then he ran desperately away from her.

Chapter

29

It was strange to him how quiet and controlled he was when he faced his grandfather. He thought he would rage and shout at him, but he was quiet and very calm.

And Peter Atwood was pale but just as quiet and calm.

"I offered Kaplan a huge sum of money to give your mother up."

"How much?"

"A million dollars."

"That is a lot of money," Jonathan said quietly.

"It is."

"And?"

"He refused it."

"Because he loved my mother?"

Atwood didn't answer.

"He did, Grandfather," Jonathan said. "With all his heart and soul."

"I believe he did," Atwood said.

"And you?" Jonathan asked. "You loved Grandmother?"

"Yes."

"Would you have given her up for a million dollars?"

"No."

"There was no money in the world that would have made you do it. None, Grandfather."

"None, Jonathan."

"Then why did you expect my father to?"

Atwood was silent.

"Because he was a Jew? And Jews love money?"

"Jonathan."

Jonathan suddenly rose from his chair. "You destroyed two people. My father and my mother. There's nothing left in her. She married a man she doesn't love. Because you wanted her to. And now she drinks too much and goes through the motions of living. You killed her, too. Why?"

He came closer to the tall, white-faced man and shouted, "Why? Tell me why?"

"You would never understand."

"Try me."

The old man shook his head and turned away. "No," he said. "No."

"Tell me."

"I did it for you."

Jonathan stared at him. "For me?"

"Yes. You. You. You, Jon." He sat down wearily and then said in a low and broken voice, "You're an Atwood, Jon. I wanted you to carry on the tradition. To take over when I was gone."

And then he repeated, "You're an Atwood."

He looked up at Jonathan with clear, cold eyes. "We go back to the beginning of this country. You and I." His face hardened. "A pure line, Jonathan."

And Jonathan thought of Carl with his bald head and military fatigues and madness in the icy blue eyes, and he saw the same madness in his grandfather's cold, commanding blue eyes.

Purity.

Ever purity.

Peter Atwood with his tailored clothes and patrician ways was no different from Carl the scabby Skinhead. The same vicious, inhuman, un-American views.

"We're Americans, Jonathan. A Kaplan doesn't belong in our line. They're outsiders. Their culture is not our culture."

"We must be pure," Jonathan said.

"We must. Or this country will go down the drain." Then he looked up at Jonathan. "You understand."

Jonathan gazed at the old man and a surge of sadness swept over him, a sadness for his grandfather and everything he stood for.

But then cold anger took over.

"I'm leaving you, Grandfather. Leaving you forever," Jonathan said.

Peter Atwood trembled.

"What difference was there between you and the Skinheads who killed my father? They did it with fists and iron bars. And you? What was your weapon?"

He choked up.

Then he spoke again, in a whisper.

"You both are murderers."

"Jon."

Jonathan walked away from him and out of the room. The voice of the old man followed him.

"Jon. Jon, don't go. Jon."

And then he heard the pleading voice no more.

Chapter
30

He stood alone at Kennedy. Stark and alone. His face grim and white.

And then an old, white-haired man approached him.

"Jonathan."

It was Walter.

"You're going away?"

"Yes."

"You couldn't come back and stay with him?"

Jonathan shook his head. "It's impossible, Walter."

"Is it?"

"We're in two different worlds. I could never again live in his. Never."

"You couldn't try?"

"No."

The old man slowly nodded. "You are in another world," he said gently.

143

He put his hand into his coat pocket and drew out a gold watch.

"Your father gave this to me years ago," he said. "I believe he hoped against forlorn hope that someday I could give it to you."

He put the watch into Jonathan's hand.

"Open it," he said.

Jonathan silently opened the back cover. Then he read the inscription. *To Jonathan Kaplan, my son.*

He heard Walter's voice.

"All through the years I let him know what was happening to you. He would ask for every detail. Every single thing about you. And he told me about himself. And how one day Jenny Mason had come into his life."

"Jenny?"

"Yes. When you called me from Seattle and told me you were returning the next day, I got in touch with her and told her where to find you in the airport. I gave her your flight number and airline. I also told her what you had said to me, that Alfred Kaplan had died before you could talk to him. Or he to you."

He paused and then went on.

"It was your father's fervent wish that someday you should meet Jenny. He was always wondering how he could arrange it. And then Death did."

Jonathan didn't speak.

"Jonathan."

"Yes?"

"Peter Atwood is leaving you his entire fortune."

"I don't want it."

"It will be yours. To do with as you wish. To him, you're an Atwood. Always and forever."

Jonathan's hand tightened around the watch but he said nothing.

"Your mother," Walter said.

"Yes?"

"Don't push her out of your life. Please, Jonathan."

"I won't," Jonathan said gently.

"She was a victim of your grandfather's bigotry just as your father was. You must always remember that. She has paid a terrible price for letting Peter Atwood do what he did. When you are older you will see things better. And you will be more forgiving of her. You will."

"I see them now, Walter."

"When you are older."

The two stood looking at each other.

Then Walter reached out his hand. It trembled.

"Good-bye, Jonathan," he said.

Jonathan embraced him and held him close. Close to his heart.

And when he let the man go, he knew that his days as an Atwood were over.

He turned and walked away.

Never looking back.

But there were tears in his eyes.

Chapter
31

It was raining in Seattle when his plane landed.

A soft, feathery rain.

He felt the rain filter into his very being, and his eyes were sad when he walked away from the baggage area and into one of the lobbies of the huge terminal.

And then he saw her.

Standing alone.

So very alone.

The pink scarf.

The large gray eyes looking so desperately to him.

"Jenny," he whispered.

She started running to him.

"Jon. Jon."

And now he held her in his arms.

Tight.

Ever so tight.

And he knew he had come home to stay.

About the Author

Jay Bennett, a master of suspense, was the first writer to win in two successive years the Mystery Writers of America's prestigious Edgar Allen Poe Award for Best Juvenile Mystery. *The Skeleton Man* was nominated for the 1986 Edgar Allan Poe Award. He is the author of many suspense novels for young adults, as well as successful adult novels, stage plays, and television scripts. His latest book with Fawcett books was *Sing Me a Death Song*. Mr. Bennett lives in Cherry Hill, New Jersey.

JAY BENNETT

Also available
at your local bookstores
from Fawcett Books.

DARK CORRIDOR

THE HAUNTED ONE

THE SKELETON MAN

SING ME A DEATH SONG